# Tomahawk Border

# Tomahawk Border

## William O. Steele

ILLUSTRATED BY
*VERNON WOOTEN*

*Colonial Williamsburg*
WILLIAMSBURG, VIRGINIA

Distributed by
*Holt, Rinehart and Winston, Inc.*
NEW YORK

*To* JOYCE *and* ALBERT BOWMAN, *for fighting the good fight along many ole buffalo trails, and to their three girls,* VICKI, BETSY, CATHY

# Contents

# Chapter 1

# The gourd-head recruit

ogers!" Captain Nicholas Flood's bellow echoed on the warm morning air. "Get out here! And make haste!"

Delk Rogers flinched. He slammed the lid of his chest and dropped to his knees to look under his bed. Where was his cap? He had worn it yesterday, he knew that. But now, on his life, he couldn't remember what he'd done with it when he'd returned to the barracks.

He scrambled to his feet and looked wildly around the room. Today was the first muster since he'd joined the rangers a week ago. He dearly wanted to make a good impression. And he didn't know what the commander would do to him if he should appear without his cap. Commander Flood didn't care what his rangers wore, just as long as they covered themselves from head to toe, hatted and booted.

And then he saw it, there in a corner. A big green gourd painted up to resemble a silly face with crossed eyes and snaggle teeth and wearing his leather cap! Delk swooped over and snatched it up and clapped it on his head. Slipping his arm into the carbine strap, he settled the gun across his back. He straightened the shoulder belt so that his sword hung properly at his side and dashed out into the sunshine.

The yard of Fort Christanna was full of people. There were traders and clerks of the fort's trading company and many Indians—

children going to the school here and what must surely be half the inhabitants of the nearby Saponi town. It seemed to Delk they were all looking at him as he rushed along with his sword banging awkwardly against his leg. He took his place at the end of the line of rangers and horses and faced the commander mounted on his gray horse.

Captain Flood glared at him, scowling like a baited bull. He certainly looked plenty fierce, even if the rangers did say he was more noise and threats than anything else. Delk shifted uneasily, expecting the worse.

"Rogers!" bawled the captain.

Delk raised his head and squared his shoulders and tried to look as if he was a veteran ranger and not the youngest one at Fort Christanna. He looked straight at Captain Flood. "Yes, sir," he answered in what he hoped was a bold voice.

"What was you lagging for in there, the last trump?" shouted the commander, letting his face swell up with anger and turn almost purple. "Promptness is a virtue that every ranger has got to have. It ain't a thing he can think about getting next year. He must have it now. And so must you! I'll not have my soldiers dallying about when I aim for them to be out here for muster. Do you hear?"

"No, sir," sang out Delk. "I . . . I mean, yes, sir!"

"Gourd head!" whispered Hurdly Lane, the man next to Delk. The boy knew they were all grinning, tickled to see the commander bullyrag him. And he guessed they must think him stupid and unfit to be a ranger along the frontier of Virginia. It was very discouraging.

Flood stared at Delk for a long minute. The August heat shimmered down into the fort yard and glanced dully off the cannons on the palisade walls. A mockingbird whirled and twirled along the ridgepole of a barrack roof, sending forth peal after peal of bubbling notes. Its joy seemed to have a mocking edge to Delk. Even the bird was tormenting him.

The ranger commander turned his eyes from Delk and swept his glance along the row of men. Now he would give them their duty assignments for the week.

But he didn't. Instead he suddenly dug his heels into his horse's side and rode ten paces past the rangers to hold an earnest conversation with Captain Hix, manager of the Indian trading company at the fort. That was just like Flood, Delk knew. He liked to make them all wait, to pretend that his affairs were more important than even the rangers, and to keep them standing about as long as he could.

The other men fell to talking quietly among themselves, mostly grumbling. But Delk was too miserable to join in their gossip. His troubles seemed to him as numerous and hateful as the many flies and gnats that flew around the horses' eyes and nostrils and made them jumpy this morning.

He was scared, in the first place. Afraid that Captain Flood would decide he was never going to make a ranger and throw him out. What would become of him then? He couldn't go back home, he just couldn't. He couldn't abide to hear his sisters' talk. Not after he'd run off without a word and joined the rangers all on his own.

But how could he make his way in the world, a sixteen-year-old boy who'd never done a thing for himself in this life? And that was his sisters' fault, for a fact. All his lifelong, since his mother died when he was less than a year old, those four women had followed him about, scolding and fussing and nagging. But all the while they were telling him to close the gate or hang up his jacket or fetch his boots in from the porch, they were doing it for him!

He'd never had to lift a hand for himself and that was the truth. Even what times he had got away from them and gone hunting or visiting or something, they'd sent old Black Cato with him, and Cato was worse than the four of them put together.

His sisters and his servants had managed to ruin him, he thought glumly. The other rangers were right to tease and torment him. Now the cap this morning—they wouldn't have had an opportunity to hide it and make fun if Delk hadn't left it lying about in the first place. If he'd remembered to put it in his chest where it belonged, all would have been well. But he knew that he had simply dropped it on some bed or table as he came into the barracks, expecting someone else to look after it.

When he'd first joined the rangers, he hadn't minded being teased, since he was the newest member and so much younger than the rest. He'd no sooner set foot in their sleeping quarters and thrown his leather cap on the table than the soldiers had gathered about. They had poked their fingers at it and one even got a stick and gave it a whack, saying, "That there's a dangerous critter and ought to be dead."

Another cried, "Kill it, quick. It's the skin of a dipper-mouth December firebug and it'll give the boy the rheumatics for certain."

"Hold on," shouted another. "It be the inside-out egg of a flying turtle. I ain't never seen one in my life before, but I'd know one anywheres. It's precious rare."

It had been sort of friendly and Delk hadn't minded. But then that very day he'd walked off and left the gate to the horse pen open. And nearly shot the commander himself because he'd forgotten his carbine was loaded when he started cleaning it. And done a half dozen other careless unthinking things.

So now the other men had turned against him, and certainly the commander didn't hold too high an opinion of him. There were so many things to remember to do and even more to remember not to do, that Delk was growing more dejected every day. Each morning he got up resolving to do better, but somehow he always managed to do some foolish thing before the sun reached the peak of the sky. And now this. He'd not doubt that this would give him another bad mark with Captain Flood.

He glanced up at the captain who was now riding slowly back toward his men and, looking very serious and thoughtful.

"He's a-trying to make up his mind whether to wear his blue shirt with the gilt buttons or his white one," muttered someone back of Delk as they all took their places. "A sack over his ugly face would be the best thing to wear," another said.

Captain Flood began to speak. "You're here for this week's duty assignments," he said. "Two men are sick and one enlistment is still unfilled so I must send out two patrols only, but I'll put three men in each one this time. Those of you ranging, be on constant guard. Let nothing escape your eyes."

His horse jumped forward with a snort and the commander paused to quiet it. The gnats and flies were fierce. Delk dropped his reins to swat at his neck. That was a mosquito and he'd gotten it.

His horse took this opportunity to walk off and he had to leap for the reins and jerk the animal back into line.

"Remember, soldiers," Captain Flood continued, "no Injun is allowed to pass through our domains and no Injun is allowed to visit any white plantation without a passport. Suspicious Injuns lurking about should be pursued through woods and deserts. Let nothing stop you till you catch them and bring them to the fort."

He coughed, shifted in his saddle, and then went on. "Governor Spotswood and all of Virginia is depending on us to protect them. The tributary Indians hereabouts is depending on us too. So, men, we must at all times do all we can for their security. We are a barrier here on the Tomahawk Border against the incursions of any foreign enemy and we must not be slack in our duties. It is the responsibility of each ranger at Fort Christanna to guard our southern frontier and if necessary guard it with your life . . ." Commander Flood's voice rose as he spoke and now he suddenly stood up in the stirrups, pointing a finger up and down the lines of rangers, and shouted, "Flesh alive and tear it! I want every jack man of you to do just that when the time comes. No shirking ever! Rangers are not cowards."

He sank back into the saddle and Delk wondered how often the rangers had listened to this very same speech. He himself had heard it, word for word, when he had first arrived here at the fort and reported to the captain. The men in the barracks had called the commander an old windbag and said he was vain and puffed up with his own importance, that the only reason there was a muster was so he could show off in front of every one at the fort. There was some truth in what they said, for Delk could see that he was enjoying himself very much.

Then Captain Flood called out the names of the three men who were to stay with him at the fort. Delk was not among them. Was he to ride with one of the ranging parties then? He hardly dared hope for such good luck. Likely he would be called aside and told to pack up his possessions and go home.

The commander turned toward the gate. "Captain Captain," he called.

A tall Indian in a striped shirt and breechclout stepped forward.

He was the head chief of the Indian town located near the fort. Delk couldn't help smiling. The others were used to the chief's odd name, but it always tickled Delk's fancy.

"Captain, you got twelve scouts ready to range?"

The chief nodded and said, "Amen." It was a word he had learned from listening to the Reverend Charles Griffin, the teacher of the Indian children. Delk reckoned he must like it for he never seemed to talk without using a sprinkling of amens.

Flood turned back toward the rangers and his eyes fell on Delk. He pulled at his beard for a moment then said, "Rogers."

"Yes, sir," Delk answered. His heart bumped again and he braced himself for the worst.

"You're raw, boy," Captain Flood went on. "You've not had enough experience on the border to fill a flea's ear. I'm going to send you out with Stryker, and mind, I want you to learn. I want you to do just as Stryker tells you. I want you to keep your ears and eyes open every hour of the day. I want you to come back here with something in your noggin besides moonbeams."

Several of the rangers snickered. But Delk didn't care. He was eager to get out in the woods. He knew he could prove his mettle in time of danger and action. Or any way, he hoped he could.

"And be on time!" thundered the Captain. "I've winked at your tardiness this muster, but it ain't to happen again, hear!" He glowered around. "Lane will be the third man."

Hurdly Lane groaned. Delk set his jaw. He'd show them all. He would be a ranger.

"Stryker, take six Injuns and range west to the warpath that crosses the Roanoke islands. Go up the warpath a bit. We don't want any Seneca lurking about causing mischief," Flood went on. Then he assigned the other three rangers their territory and added one last order, "Be back in four days. If you're forced to stay out longer, send an express."

He drew himself up and his command rang out, "Range-eeerrrs, mount!"

With a flick of the wrist Delk threw his reins over the horse's head and grabbed the saddle pommel. He put his left foot in the stirrup and swung himself up. But something happened. He wasn't

an assignment the thirteen rangers here had, they were so few against so many enemies. Yet Delk was confident that he, for one, was worthy of such a responsibility. He knew that he was going to do his very best.

In his mind's eye he saw himself riding across a flat land where Indians stood as thick and tall as trees. He rode right into them whirling his sword and shouting and shooting and scattering all of them before him in terror, just as he imagined his father must have done years ago when he was with the county militia.

He twisted in the saddle to get one last look at the fort and his knee knocked a pistol from its holster. It fell to the ground and the horse stepped on it. He'd forgotten to buckle down the flap. He'd have to remember after this.

He jumped off and got the pistol, put it in the holster at the front part of the saddle, buckled the flap on it, and then secured the one on the other side. He checked the rest of his equipment. His cartridges were in the pouch at his right hip, his sword and carbine were in place. This time he was ready. This time he'd thought of everything, he was almost certain.

Urging his horse into a gallop, he passed in among the trees after the others. He was quite happy. There would be three or four days of ranging and he hoped to enjoy it. He'd left behind him forever the pesky chatter of four sisters, the worrying over tobacco prices, the dull day-to-day routine of farm work. He sang a snatch of a song that his youngest sister used to sing about a bold soldier:

> He drew his sword and pistol and caused them to rattle;
> The lady held his horse while the soldier fought the battle.

Ranger Delk Rogers, a soldier bold, a fighter of great battles! He rode on, grinning to himself.

# Chapter 2

# Guarding the border with sword and cap

*J*t was the second night on the range. Delk lay on the ground with his head pillowed on his saddle watching the Roanoke River ripple peacefully against the end of a little island and then go frothing off over the shallows. The sun was setting and the little waves were rose pink on the crests and blood red in the troughs. Along the opposite bank the shadows huddled under the trees. A dove called drowsily and the jarflies rasped out their final songs.

Hurdly bent over the fire and pulled a leg off the turkey browning over the coals. "Best have a bite more," he called out to Delk.

Delk shook his head. He'd already eaten most of a turkey all by himself. The Indians were mighty hunters; the ranging party had not yet had to eat a mouthful of the hardtack and salt-beef rations they'd brought in their saddlebags. They'd had deer meat last night and turkey and fish tonight.

"Queer thing about being out here," Hurdly went on, wiping his mouth with the back of his hand, "a body can just eat and eat. I ain't much hand for eating back at the fort, not the way them Injun women cook our food. But out here I can eat my weight mighty nigh every time we stop."

"I reckon I've ate more these past two days than I eat in a week customary," Delk said. "It must be . . ." He almost said it was because he was away from his sisters that he had such an appetite, but

11

he caught himself in time. No need of letting Hurdly know about his past life. "It must be all the riding," he added quickly.

"Captain Captain and his braves keep us in a gracious plenty of game," Hurdly commented. "They're better hunters than fighters, I'll say that." He went back to sit beside Stryker, and Delk went on staring at the darkening water and thinking.

This range hadn't been the way he'd thought it would be at all. If Flood expected him to learn anything from Stryker, he was mistaken. For Stryker had left the rest of the party soon after they set out from the fort. He'd only rejoined them tonight at supper time and now sat under the trees looking ill tempered.

However Delk had learned more than a little. For Hurdly Lane had sent him riding all over the countryside. He didn't know why it seemed to fall his lot to investigate every thicket and every faint trail, but it had. He was always the one who had to go, alone and unknowing, to search out the enemy. Lane hadn't even sent one of the Indians with him.

He supposed Lane wanted him to get used to being on his own and to using his head about following tracks and riddling out signs. Delk appreciated these chances. He hadn't come across a single indication of danger, and he'd taken much pleasure in riding alone among the big trees and over the hillsides. It was very different country from what he was used to, even the Indian old fields, set in the middle of forest and grown up in grass as high as his horse's withers. Of course, he had gotten lost lots, and Hurdly hadn't liked that.

There was a sound close by, a horse crunching stalks of cane, and Delk looked up to see his own Nuck standing at the edge of the river. Poor old Nuck, last week a harrow horse and now a ranger's mount. He must be confounded by the change—and Delk's sisters must be ireful at him for going off with the animal.

They might even, he thought uneasily, send the sheriff after him for stealing Nuck. But that was nonsense, they'd never see him dragged off to prison. He hoped they weren't too angry with him. He knew they'd be worried, for not one of them thought he had sense enough to buckle his own boots. Or at least they'd never behaved as if they thought so, always running behind him to pick up and fetch and carry.

If his father had lived, he guessed things would have been different. But his father had died so long ago that he barely remembered him, and his sisters, the oldest a dozen years his elder, had devoted all their lives to telling him what to do and how to do it—and then doing it for him.

He glanced up again at Nuck, and then sprang to his feet. He'd forgot once again to hobble the horse. It was the merest luck Nuck hadn't strayed off. Delk hoped the others hadn't noticed.

But they had. "Gourd head," jeered Lane. "Reckon you mean to make the Senecas a present of him."

Delk didn't answer but hurried to grab Nuck and lead him away from the river. The horse seemed to be limping and he wondered if Nuck had thrown a shoe. It was something he had to watch for, one more thing on his long list to remember to do. He inspected Nuck's hoofs. Working in the sandy soil of the farm, the horse had never needed shoes and Delk had felt sorry for him when he'd learned that shoeing was necessary. But the fort blacksmith had done his work well and Nuck didn't seem to mind. All was well so he hobbled him.

"It's a mighty change for both of us, ain't it?" Delk whispered, rubbing the velvety nose.

It had all been so sudden. One day he'd found his father's old sword and carbine and a pair of pistols in a chest in the back of the storeroom. He'd tried to picture his father riding with the militia of Charles City County, holding a smoking pistol or slashing about with his sword. It pleased him to think that his father had been a gay, dashing cavalryman, and he decided to clean the weapons and take them to his room, no matter what his sisters might say.

And the very next day his sister Arabella's beau, George Arrington, had told them that Captain Flood was about the countryside looking for recruits for his rangers and not having much luck.

It hadn't taken Delk any time to make up his mind. Less than a week after that he and Nuck were gone from the farm, run off with his father's arms to join the rangers. It might be that some day they'd be back. In the meantime George could marry Arabella and try to run the farm if he liked. Delk could have told him he didn't stand a chance with those four bossy women.

Captain Flood hadn't wanted to enlist Delk, a boy just turned sixteen, knowing less than nothing about the work he'd be required to do.

"He must have been desperate to take me," thought Delk.

But what did the captain expect? The farmers of the colony were too busy tending to their plantations to enlist. And anyway in four months, in December, the rangers would be disbanded. The Indian trading company would take over the fort and the frontier guard duty. Delk prayed that in these four months something would come about that would make it unnecessary for him to go back to the plantation.

He couldn't figure what it would be. Something wonderful. Something like rescuing the governor from a runaway coach. Delk pictured himself riding up to snatch the reins of the frightened horses and drag them to a stop, he could see the governor, pale faced and periwig askew, leaning from the coach to ask him his name and then give him a reward—a sack of gold, or a piece of fine land.

"Not likely," he muttered to himself. He'd never get a chance to come near the governor. And chances were he'd spoil such an opportunity by forgetting something, if he did. He picked up a stone and skimmed it over the water, and a big white heron, gliding along, twisted its head to look at the flat rock hopping and splashing across the river and then flew on.

"Come and set, boy," called Hurdly, and Delk walked through the twilight and sat down with the other two rangers, so anxious to get rid of his own thoughts that he was almost glad of their company.

"You got to remember to hobble your horse," growled Stryker. "This is Injun country."

"Surely is," agreed Hurdly. "You seen that path back there, not a stone's throw from this camp? That's a warpath, comes all the way down from New York Colony. It crosses the river here and goes way off down into Catawba country. Them Senecas hate Catawbas worse than sin, and they travel this way all the time, just spoiling for a fight. This here's Virginia land and they got no right to come on it. But they don't pay no heed to such as that. I reckon you know all this, howsomever?"

Delk shook his head. Of course he knew it, he had heard it all from the men at the fort. Still he listened to Lane like he was a knee-high child, hearing it for the first time. He didn't mean to rile Hurdly, not at all.

"They don't mind coming over to Fort Christanna and picking up a Saponi scalp if they can. Or even a white man's. Why," Hurdly said, glancing quickly at Delk, "I mind not twenty miles from here, me and an old friend was out hunting one fallish day and the Senecas got him. They'd have got me, but I clumb a tree and they couldn't spy me out. Poor old Jones," he shook his head. "They killed him right there with me hiding in the tree. I could see it all. He hollered all day and all night. It was terrible. The Senecas is the meanest Injuns there is."

Stryker grunted.

"They pull fingernails and burn pine splinters under your skin and do most awful things," Hurdly continued. "They know how to make it hurt the most and keep you alive the longest. Once we come along here and found a Catawba they'd just had their fun with. Wasn't nothing left of him but little pieces, but all them little pieces was still warm, he'd been dead such a little spell."

Stryker spat into the fire. Delk said nothing.

"They're sly too," Hurdly went on. "Hardly ever leave any sign about for anybody to see. I wager there's half a dozen of 'em now out there in the woods. Maybe more, quietly watching everything we do."

Delk forced himself not to look over his shoulder into the blackness all about them. He didn't really think there were Indians out there. But, for a fact, you couldn't know for certain.

Hurdly slid his eyes first around at Delk and then toward Stryker. He cleared his throat. "Now me and Stryker was just saying," he nodded earnestly, "that we'd best post extra guards tonight, being we're so near the trail and all."

"Ain't the Injuns along to do the guarding?" Delk asked. He looked around to where they had their own campfire. Two sat cross legged playing some game, the rest slept. They certainly didn't seem worried about Senecas sneaking about.

Hurdly shook his head. "You can't trust these tributary Injuns, you know that," he answered. "When it comes to a real pinch, us rangers has got to depend on ourself. Now me and Stryker has talked things over, and we're going to let you have first watch, for that is the easiest time for a body to stay awake. Anyway, Injuns'll be more liable to attack at dawn and us old-timers will be watching then."

Delk said nothing. Surely this was a trick, a joke. Hurdly must have planned the whole thing to get Delk out by himself in the woods so he could scare the liver and lights out of him, sneaking up and pretending to be a Seneca.

Hurdly stood up. "Now I'll show you where I want you," he told the boy. "Get your cap and come with me."

"My cap?" asked Delk. "Whatever for?" The night was warm, there wasn't any point in wearing a headpiece.

"If you're going to die," explained Hurdly solemnly, "you got to die like a real ranger, covered from one end to 'tother, like the captain likes us to be."

Now Delk felt sure it must be a joke. Hurdly must figure he was too new and green to catch on. He'd show him. He fetched his cap and his sword and carbine and pistols.

"Now you just lay them pieces right down," said Hurdly hastily. Delk grinned a little to himself, but he laid aside the pistols and the carbine. "You know Captain Flood don't want us killing Injuns. He wants 'em captured and brought back alive. You can use your sword for that. If you had one of them pistols with you, you'd fire it for sure, and dead Injuns ain't no use to the captain."

They set off through the trees.

"A ranger leads a mighty hard life," said Hurdly mournfully. "Danger and fighting all the time. I wouldn't be here myself except for I got drunk and Captain Flood took advantage of my good nature and signed me up. It was along about the time the Yamassee Injuns started a little war down in Carolina and the commander, he figured it would spread to Virginia. Never did though, and I sure was glad."

At last Hurdly stopped. "This is it," he said. "Moon'll be up in a while, and you can see a good piece up and down the path from here then."

"All right," replied Delk. He guessed one place was as good as another to be scared by Hurdly Lane.

"Now you just forget them things I was talking about back yonder," Lane added in a smirking voice. "All that about burning and killing and Injun meanness. A ranger, well, he's got his duty to do. He can't let his mind dwell on such things. He's got risks to run and it don't profit him a shilling to think on a thing but his duties. So you just wait right here and if you see an Injun, get him."

"I sure will," said Delk in a steady voice. He knew Hurdley was grinning to himself in the dark.

"Well, good luck, young 'un," said Hurdly, and the night swallowed him up.

Delk settled back resignedly against a tree with the sword across his lap. This was just something he'd have to put up with, he knew. But he was tired and sleepy, and it was irksome to have to be out here in the dark just so Hurdly Lane could have his little fun. He hoped that the ranger would come soon else he'd never be able to keep awake. And he wanted to be ready and waiting to give as good as he got.

He yawned. The songs of the katydids were soothing, and a breeze, cool and caressing, had come up. It was peaceful and pleasant. He yawned again.

Something snapped among the bushes behind him and Delk whirled. But nothing happened. It wasn't Hurdly then. What could it have been? It was possible that there were Indians around him. It was always possible. After all, if there wasn't a danger from Indians, the rangers wouldn't be out in the woods at all.

Delk stared all around in the blackness. He tried so hard to see through the shadows that his eyeballs ached. When *would* the moon come up? Was that really something moving in the dark? Did he hear an arm brushing against the undergrowth, a foot pressed to the bare earth in the trail?

He was certain he heard breathing. He held his own breath, listening for all he was worth, while the little wind whispered in the leaves and cooled the sweat on his forehead.

A night bird called and Delk jumped. There was another sound, like the ring of metal on stone. It must be the ranger. A man as big as Hurdly could hardly hope to move quietly through the woods. The minutes passed and nothing came.

Suddenly all the katydids close to him were strangely silent. He stood, pressing his back tight against the tree. Somebody was here in the woods with him. Somebody had disturbed the creatures. He rested his hand on the hilt of his sword, but the weapon gave him no comfort. Even if he could draw it from the scabbard, it wouldn't be much good to him in a real fight. He'd never used a sword for one thing, and for another this one was so dull and rusty he might as well be fighting with a wooden spoon.

He groaned to himself. One of the things he'd meant to do before he left the fort was polish up that sword and put a keener edge to the blade. He'd truly meant to. He didn't know how it had come to slip his mind.

The katydids rasped on once again, and still he waited alone and skittish. He thought more and more of Indians, flames licked at his feet and he all but hollered out at the pain he imagined he felt. He wished he could put torture and suffering out of his mind.

Now the moon was coming up. A faint glow fell among the trees and Delk was relieved. At least he could see. He slumped at ease against the trunk. And right then something seized him by the elbow. In spite of all his resolution Delk howled in fear. Turning fast he swung the sword and scabbard with all his might. It crashed into flesh and bone and went flying from his hands!

# Chapter 3

# *The surprised Seneca*

*A* dark figure collapsed at the foot of the tree. Delk leaned forward and peered into the shadows. "Hurdly!" he cried. "Be you all right? I never went to—you hadn't ought to frighten me so Hurdly!"

The shape on the ground stirred and staggered to its feet. Delk put out a hand to help and then drew it back in horror. For the moonlight, striking suddenly down through a gap in the trees, fell on a cruel face, one hook nosed and savage and merciless. But it was the glint on the blade of the scalping knife raised overhead that sent Delk scooting.

He slid around to the other side of the trunk as silently and swiftly as a lizard. The red man followed, and then for a few minutes they dodged back and forth around the big tree trunk with Delk stumbling over the roots and just managing to keep out of reach of that slashing sharp blade.

But the Indian was too quick for him. Feinting a lunge toward the boy, he dashed quickly in the opposite direction and grabbed him by the shoulder. Delk knocked away his hand but lost his footing and went crashing back against the trunk. The knife flashed above him once again.

In sheer terror and desperation and without a thought of anything but staying clear of that thin, wicked-looking blade, Delk snatched off his cap and lashed out. It smacked across the Indian's face and the brave cried out. Delk was almost as surprised as the red man, but not entirely. He whipped the cap back and forth, raining blows across the warrior's eyes and nose. The Indian let the knife fall from his hand, covered his head with his arms, and sank to his knees. Delk just went right on slapping and slapping, too scared to stop.

Finally he remembered to yell. "Help!" he bawled. "Hurdly. Help, help!"

Every time he hollered out the Indian rose up and then Delk had to beat harder and faster, raining blows on his head and shoulders and chest furiously to keep him down.

"Help!" Swat, swat, whack! "Help! Hurdly!" Whomp, thump, swat!

"Hang on, boy, we're coming!"

It was Hurdly's voice, and he was close. In a minute he and Stryker and two of the Saponi were standing beside Delk. The Indians had cane torches held high.

"Great day in the morning!" exclaimed Hurdly and he whistled softly. For the brave's face was a terrifying sight, bruised and bleeding, with a great lump on one side of his head and his eyes already beginning to swell shut. "You done all this with your plain bare hands?"

Delk shook his head and tried to quiet the thumping of his heart. At last he managed to squeak out, "No, I done it with my cap, mostly. Only that big knot on his head, that was the sword." He stopped and then went on in a shamed voice. "I couldn't get the sword out of the scabbard. I . . . I forgot to clean it and it was stuck fast."

"Well, forevermore," Hurdly went on, still gazing at the Indian. "Well, I knowed you was a fighter, the minute I laid eyes on you. You got a fighter's way of holding your head. You just got a fighter's cold look. Oh, now this beats all, don't it, Stryker?"

Stryker grunted. It was the way he usually answered questions. He said less than any man Delk had ever seen.

"Now, nobody wouldn't believe this if I was to tell 'em," went on Hurdly. "This here boy, hardly got his growth yet, and he done whipped a Seneca with nothing but a leather cap! One of the fiercest Injuns in creation. It beats all!"

Delk fingered the cap. It was true, of course. It really had happened, even if it seemed like a dream to him, even if it was the kind of thing nobody would believe, as Hurdly said. He looked down at the cap with a certain respect and then settled it comfortably on his head. It felt fine up there.

But he wasn't taken in by Hurdly Lane's bragging on him. He knew what Hurdly was doing, trying to make everybody forget that he was the one who had risked Delk's life for a foolish joke, sending him out here to stand on the warpath alone and without proper weapons.

Delk didn't really hold it against him. If he hadn't been the thoughtless boy he was, he'd have sneaked back to camp right behind Hurdly and let the joke be on Lane.

In a way he was glad now he hadn't crept back. He'd have missed this chance to be a hero. And it made him feel pretty good, anyway, to know he could hold his own in a fight, even against odds. He wished his sisters could know about it. How they'd marvel.

Captain Captain pointed a finger at the man lying on the ground. "Seneca!" he said loudly. "Mean, plenty mean, amen!"

"Tie him up," ordered Stryker. "Get him back to camp."

He leaned over as if to jerk the Indian to his feet and then suddenly stayed his hand. Instead he reached down and slid something from beneath the red man's body. It was a straight stick, square and oddly notched into alternating black and red sections. Stryker pressed it against his leg, casually, as though he'd hardly noticed what he was doing.

"Get him back to camp," he repeated and strode off into the dark.

"What was that he found?" Delk wanted to know.

"Him war stick, amen," Captain Captain said. "One chief send. Far-away chief get stick. Cut off notch every day. One notch, one broken day. Stick all gone, take warpath."

"A sort of express," thought Delk, "and a right clever one."

"'Twas?" asked Hurdly, looking ill at ease. "Well, maybe, if you say so, Captain Captain."

"A war stick?" queried Delk. "How come Stryker tried to hide it from us?"

"Oh, him," replied Lane vaguely. "He's a queer one. Ain't no telling what he does things for."

Delk watched the two Saponi tie up the prisoner and then shove him roughly off through the trees. "If there's going to be a war, we ought to do something about it," he objected. It was exciting to think about. A real fight and this time he could use his weapons instead of a silly leather cap.

"There ain't fixing to be no war *now*," said Hurdly sharply, as they set out for camp. "Ain't nobody going to get that war stick, so can't nobody go to war. Anyway, this Injun'll never tell us where he was headed. Most likely, though, he was going down south among his kinfolks, the Tuscaroras. Senecas like to get together with them and make trouble. Ain't nothing to get upset about. Us rangers can handle anything they're a mind to try."

He grinned and clapped Delk on the shoulder. "Anyway, ain't no Injun tribe going to be willing to fight us now," he said, "since we got the fiercest fighter this side of the equator."

Maybe he was and then again maybe not, Delk told himself. To whip a Seneca and stop an Indian war in one night with a leather cap was a deed to brag about, but it wasn't real honest-to-goodness fighting. As he slipped into his blanket, he couldn't help wondering whether he'd be brave and fierce when bullets and tomahawks and arrows were flying all about him and soldiers were bleeding and dying all around. It'd take a real battle for him to know whether he was a horse soldier or not.

A strange thing happened between that camp and Fort Christanna. The Seneca warrior, who had been Delk's prisoner, somehow became Stryker's prisoner. Hurdly hardly spoke again of what a brave fighter Delk was or how wonderful it had been to capture an Indian brave with only a leather cap. Nobody seemed to think this exploit was anything Captain Flood would care to hear.

It made Delk mad, but not much. He would like to be thought of as a clever and courageous Indian fighter, but in his head he knew it wasn't true. It had been luck and despair that captured the Seneca, not boldness and skill, and he knew it. He was probably better off not claiming credit for the deed, he told himself. He had troubles enough without trying to keep up the pretense that he was a fighter.

Right now for instance. Captain Flood right this minute was bellowing about the dunderhead who had left an axe lying in the mud when the stockade was mended this morning. Delk knew who that dunderhead was. When he'd set out to do that task, he'd made a solemn vow to himself to do it right, not to neglect the least little thing, and especially he'd sworn to remember to put all the tools away properly.

He groaned to himself. What was the matter with him? For just as he'd finished nailing in the last peg, one of the traders of the Indian company had ridden in with news of troubles among the tribes to the south. Delk had run to listen with the rest, and not till this minute had he thought again of the axe lying by the log pickets.

Maybe his sisters were right to do everything for him. Maybe it was just hopeless for him to do anything but go home and once again let them tend to him—this time for the rest of his life.

He took the commander's tongue-lashing with bent head. He deserved it, he knew, but worse yet was the feeling that he had tried so hard and failed again.

For punishment he had to wash and curry Captain Flood's horse. He was glad the assignment wasn't guarding the prisoner. Whenever Delk passed the tiny gaol built under one of the gun platforms, he saw that there was one body who hadn't forgotten who had made that capture—the Seneca himself. He glared out of his little barred window at the people in the fort yard, hating them all. But when Delk passed, the man's brown hands grasped the bars tightly and the loathing that shone out of his eyes was enough to scald Delk's hide and burn his marrow.

Delk avoided going that way if he could, but he worried all the time about the gaol. The door was a heavy wooden one with a strong lock. It looked secure enough, but the clapboard sides of the cell looked weak and even rotten in a place or two.

"He's going to bust out of there some night and come find me," Delk thought unhappily. "And I'll be lucky if slitting my throat is all he does to me."

He tried hard not to let on that he was uneasy, but many a dark night he lay awake listening for the sound of Indian footsteps. And one day he couldn't stand it any longer. He had to find out if the prisoner was going to spend the next year glaring out of that window, or what.

"Hurdly," he asked, "what'll Flood do with the Seneca?"

"Oh, he'll have him roasted one of these Sundays," answered Lane. "Put a pumpkin in his mouth and he'll feed him to the whole fort. Be enough left over to fry the next morning, I'll lay."

Delk grinned, "Aw, come on," he said. "What will happen to him? Tell the truth for once, Hurdly."

"Tell the truth and shame the devil, that's what my ma was always saying to me," mused Hurdly. He mopped his face with a rag he'd been using to clean his carbine.

"Well, tell it now," urged Delk.

"He'll end up in Williamsburg, likely," Hurdly said at last. "That's where the last one went. Anyhow, it ain't no concern of yours."

Delk nodded but he thought, "Well, I wish this one would hurry up and get there."

That very night, after supper, Stryker walked into the sleeping quarters and said roughly, "Rogers, be ready by sunup tomorrow. You'll be making a journey."

"A journey?" cried Delk. "Where to?"

"Williamsburg," replied Stryker shortly. "To take the prisoner. With the commander and Captain Captain."

He turned on his heel and left Delk gaping. "How come I was the one?" he asked Lane. "How come did I get picked?"

"Now that I'd like to know," said one of the other rangers bitterly. "A gourd-green young 'un. I figured me to be the one to go, and I was minded to pleasure myself whilst I was there just a heap."

"And that's why you ain't going," Hurdly said. "Last time Flood went to Williamsburg, the men with him was ever in trouble, at the taverns and in the streets. And Flood didn't like it. He likes to spend the time shaking a toe with the ladies and being a gentleman. He wants somebody with him this time who'll keep his head and not get drunk and get in a brawl. He don't like having to haul his rangers out of gaol."

Delk was troubled. "I . . . I don't know," he said. "It might be I'll not know what to do. I might get muddled up and let the prisoner escape."

"Not with the Injun along," Hurdly pointed out. "Captain Captain hates Senecas worse than you do and he'll see he gets to the dungeon, never fear."

He spat and then grinned at Delk. "But this ain't going to make Stryker love you," he added. "I know for a fact he aimed to make this journey. He's got something he's itching to do in Williamsburg. Or on the way. Or on the road back, maybe. Anyhow, he did dearly plan to go, and when you get back with that supply of powder, he's just likely to blow you up with it."

Delk still stood there frowning. He was scared, though he hated to say so, even to himself. He was afraid he couldn't be trusted to take care of this prisoner, that in his careless way he might forget to keep the Indian tied up properly or something.

"Oh, aye, Stryker'll be after you," Lane went on. "So you make merry in the town whilst you can. Tell you what, I've got a penny put by and I'll lend it to you, so's you can have some money to spend in the grog shops. Come along, now, I'll help you shine up your pistols and get ready. You ain't got too much time."

Delk nodded and tried to look pleased. But he was still scared. "Pray nothing goes wrong," he muttered to himself. "For that Injun has his eye on my scalp and wants it worse than life!"

## Chapter 4

# Off to Williamsburg

*D*elk led Nuck and the three pack horses off the James River ferry and across the muddy, shell-strewn bank. Sea gulls whirled about him, shrieking and fighting. He tied the horses at the edge of a pine grove where they could nibble on the clumps of marsh grass. Then he walked a little way into the woods and dropped to the soft cushion of needles and stretched out on his back. The sky was a fiery blue, but none of the summer heat reached him here under these giant trees.

There were cries from the ferrymen and the boat started back across the river. The James was wide here and it'd be some time before the commander and his horse and the two Indians joined him. He lay for a long time listening to the slup-slup of water and watching through the pine branches stray twists of clouds go hurrying by. His eyelids began to drop.

He sat up quickly. It would never do to sleep here in the middle of the day, only eight miles from Williamsburg. Somebody might steal the horses. Or the commander might catch him and be mad.

This was the widest river he'd ever seen. But it was dull—just water. If he could just glimpse a big, ocean-going vessel or one of the fighting ships of the British navy, it would be grand. As it was, there was nothing but the ferryboat and bright dancing waves.

He gazed downstream toward Jamestown. He could see little of it from here, but coming across the river, he had seen a bit of the church tower through the trees. The ferryman told him that most of the inhabitants had moved to Williamsburg and all that was left of the town was the church, a court house, and a few brick buildings. Even the fort was in ruins.

He stretched lazily and yawned and yawned. He'd done a great heap of riding since they'd left Fort Christanna a day and a half ago. He thought how right Hurdly's forecast had been, for Delk had certainly not had to guard the prisoner. The journey had been easy enough for him.

Captain Captain had put the Seneca on one of the pack horses, one foot tied to the other underneath the animal. While the prisoner rode, the Saponi chief had trotted alongside him.

Delk couldn't understand why Captain Captain didn't ride, and he had been only more mystified by the Saponi's words. "Horse cripple," he'd said. "Me run. Be fine. Legs fine."

At the end of yesterday's journey when they stopped by a spring to camp for the night, Delk had understood. The Seneca got down off his horse and he could barely stand, much less walk. He was unaccustomed to riding and his legs were so galled that they were raw and bleeding in several places.

"Horse no good for Indian. Amen," Captain Captain told Delk. "Horse cripple Indian bad." He pointed to the Seneca's legs. "Him much crippled. Not run away. You see?"

Delk nodded, grinning.

"You no worry about Seneca? No worry, amen?" Captain Captain added.

"Amen, I won't worry," laughed Delk.

And he hadn't, not last night nor today either. He'd just ridden along listening to the commander tell how all the great men of the colony always invited him to their balls, for he was such a fine dancer that their wives demanded his presence at these gaieties. Delk was thoroughly sick of Nicholas Flood.

The ferry returned at last and while the commander paid for their passage, Captain Captain pushed the prisoner toward Delk. The Seneca's face was impassive, but he couldn't hide the fact that he was still lame and walked along, spraddle-legged and stiff.

"Him still cripple," Captain Captain told the boy. "Horse strong medicine for Indian."

The chief was so tickled with himself that he had forgotten to throw in one of his amens, Delk noticed. The boy was relieved that all had gone so well. Captain Captain had brought along only a bow and a quiver of arrows, and the commander had bothered to bring nothing but his pistols. But they were stored away in his saddlebags, wrapped in fine wool to keep them clean and shining.

"And now, thanks be, there are only a few more miles to go," Delk thought when they were all mounted and ready to leave.

As they started off along the rutted, sandy road, Captain Flood announced, "Well, my boy, we're almost there. Virginia's wonderful capitol. And they're waiting for me." He patted the small traveler's chest tied behind his saddle. "My dancing shoes are shined and ready, though I've often wondered," he paused and held out one foot toward the boy, "I've often wondered what the good ladies would do if I appeared at their ball at Green Spring plantation wearing my spurs." He turned and smiled at the boy, "Wouldn't that be a keg of sweet-meats?"

Delk didn't answer. He didn't have to, he'd found out on this journey. The commander asked questions of him, but he never waited for an answer and really didn't want one. All he wanted was somebody to listen. Delk sighed and placed his carbine across his lap for comfort. It was going to be a long eight miles.

But it turned out that Delk and the pack horses were too slow a company for the commander. He dashed ahead impatiently and was waiting for them at the edge of town.

"Come on, Rogers, hurry," he cried when the group came in sight. "You're going to damnify my chances of getting to Green Spring tonight. Hurry, now."

There was no use trying to explain to the commander that Nuck was not going to be hurried for any ball or for any other occasion, however grand. The old horse had sensed that the end of the journey was near and no amount of urging by Delk was going to make him speed along now. He was a very sensible horse.

So the commander cantered ahead, calling over his shoulder as he pointed off through the trees, "There's the College of William and Mary." Delk had a glimpse of red brick and that was all. He meant to come back later and take a good look.

"Now here we are on the Duke of Gloucester Street, the very heart of things!" cried the captain as they came onto a wide, dusty street.

Here and there a coach, a calash, or a chariot poked along at a sensible pace. Delk had never seen such fine vehicles, not even at a wedding. People in Williamsburg must be rich and grand indeed, thought Delk, and had to turn his eyes away from the spinning wheels of a very fine chaise before he got dizzy.

The commander was sitting tall and straight in his saddle, his eyes were bright and his color high. "Heigh, ho! Ain't this grand, boy? Ain't this elegant? Oh, Lord, I can't for the life of me think how I bear living at that dull fort. Make haste, make haste!"

Delk noticed that he and the captain hardly merited a glance from the townspeople, but many did stop to stare curiously at the naked savages, the mounted Seneca whose prideful dignity still showed through the dust of travel and the straight-back, free-striding Captain Captain.

Nevertheless the commander bowed and bowed to every carriage, sure that if he hadn't already met the occupants he soon would. He kept pointing out to Delk houses where he'd been invited to tea or to a party. "There's Bruton Parish Church," he cried. "And over yonder's the magazine where we'll pick up the powder."

Delk knew his own eyes were round with wonder. His sisters had often told him about Williamsburg's many marvels. They had planned that he should go, next month, next fall, next year. Somehow something had always interfered, too much work to be done, the horse lame, too little money, always something to keep him on the plantation.

Delk hadn't cared. He hadn't somehow been able to picture what the town was like. Even now it hardly seemed real, so many people, so much color, such a great bustling about. He stared at the fine clapboard and brick houses, with the neat walkways, their gardens trimmed and clipped and cared for as though the bushes were fine horses. He gaped at the shops with their bright signs and their glistening windows displaying all kinds of stuffs. He could hardly believe his eyes.

"Now, there, Rogers, there's the capitol, that commodious pile,"

babbled Captain Flood on reaching the other end of the Duke of Gloucester Street. "There's where all our laws are made and taxes laid and collected and monies dispensed. There's a heap of very powerful men in and out of there every day."

Delk didn't know a great deal about laws and taxes, but the building was the largest he'd ever seen. It was built of bricks, with many windows and a little skinny white cupola on the top. It was certainly grand. Delk kept turning his head to look back at it. Once the sun caught all the windows so that a gold light bathed the place, and Delk thought that was what a grand and noble castle must look like.

The buildings were handsome and the people were bright as peacocks, but the streets were hardly better than the trail they had been riding, Delk thought. They were sandy, rough and rutted where the summer's drought had dried up the water. He wondered what happened to the fine people of Williamsburg and their beautiful carriages in the rainy season.

They came at last to the gaol. Delk was left to hold the horses while the others took the prisoner inside. The Seneca flashed the boy one final look of corroding hatred before he disappeared into the prison. Delk sighed with relief.

He settled down to a long wait, knowing Captain Flood and how he liked to talk. But he'd forgotten that ball, so it was only a few minutes before Flood came rushing out and mounted his horse. "Governor Spotswood will be pleased with our vigilance along the border," he said to nobody in particular. He wheeled his horse and started off, then drew up short.

"Rogers, I'm off now to get a room at Marot's Ordinary," he said. "You and Captain Captain will stay at my cousin's place. Captain Captain knows the way, he's stayed there before. Since your wants be few and simple, you'll find it a dandy spot to camp there in the meadow. Best water in town."

Delk thought his sisters would have been indignant to know that he was sleeping outdoors while the commander took a tavern room. Only one person was allowed expense money for bringing a prisoner to Williamsburg, and he'd not expected any free meals and goose-feather bed. Anyway, he'd far rather be with Captain Captain sheltering under the trees than with Nicholas Flood in a smelly room.

"We've got to leave tomorrow afternoon with the powder, so mind now, Rogers, keep up with them animals. No unlatched gates," the commander cautioned. "Meet me with the horses two hours past noon at the magazine. We'll load and head back to the fort."

He frowned darkly as though he hated to think about leaving, but then his face brightened and he said, "Ah, but I must go get ready for the ball. Huzzah!" He dashed away.

Delk glanced at the sun, low in the west over the town. By the time he and the chief got to the Flood meadow and watered the horses, rubbed them down, and turned them loose, it'd be dark for sure. They'd have their meal of dried venison and corn, and then Delk meant to roll into his blanket and go to sleep. He was tired. Let the commander rejoice in the gaiety of balls; Delk preferred a good night's sleep.

"And I reckon you do too, huh, Nuck," he asked the horse, "after all this traveling you've done?"

As he headed him down a side street behind the chief and some townspeople hurrying home to an evening meal, he gave Nuck an affectionate pat. He loved him in spite of his plodding ways and wouldn't trade him for any of the fine bays and grays he'd seen in Williamsburg. Not even for that one there, tied in front of a house, a spirited and beautiful chestnut, with one white foot.

A boy was speaking gently to the horse, a little boy with a curiously old and wizened face. No, it couldn't be a boy, it must be a dwarf, mused Delk. The little man stroked the horse's muzzle and the animal seemed to understand and enjoy the words he was whispering. The tiny man began to fumble at the bridle when suddenly the door to the house flew open and a woman rushed out screaming, "Thief! Thief!"

The little man looked up, startled and then slipped under the horse's head and fled down the street.

In a flurry of skirts and scarves the woman flounced down the steps of the house and into the street. "Stop him! Stop that thief!" she shrieked.

But the little man had long since disappeared dodging between two buildings. The woman turned and surveyed the bystanders beating her riding whip against her long blue skirt.

"Why didn't one of you stop him?" she cried angrily. "There he was, trying to steal my horse, and you didn't move a finger to stop him. Rabble! Rabble!"

She strode up to where Delk had reined to a stop and sat watching all the commotion in astonishment. It had not appeared to him that the man was trying to steal the horse.

"A great hulking boy like you, just sitting there always letting thieves get away," she yelled. Her face was crimson with rage. "And you even have a pistol and gun! Oh, what is the world coming to? None of you is worth a thrip any more." And suddenly she raised her whip and brought it sharply down on Delk's leg twice, rap, rap!

She turned and flew back into the house. Several of the bystanders giggled. Delk's cheeks burned, and he rubbed his leg softly with the heel of his hand. What a lunatic!

"Injun men beat women, amen. Injun women not beat men," said Captain Captain gravely. "Injun women got good manners."

Delk gave him a sour look. Who cared what Indian women had or hadn't? But one thing was certain, as far as he was concerned, Captain Flood could live in Williamsburg and go to balls every night, but Delk would be glad to see the fort again!

# Chapter 5

# Jamie Pigg

*W*hen Delk awoke the following morning, he could hear the far-off rumbling of thunder. Overhead the sky was gray. Clouds billowed up over the trees. He lay watching the wind sway the oak branches and turn the leaves. Suddenly hail came rattling across the town, pelting the houses and the trees and hopping about the pasture frightening the horses. Delk sheltered his head with his arms, but only a pellet or two came through his cover of branches and in a few minutes it stopped.

Captain Captain had gone, taking his bow and arrows with him. Delk wished the Indian had taken him along, but he didn't know how he'd pass the day till midafternoon when he had to meet the commander. He was a little uneasy about going down into town by himself. Besides the chief had been to Williamsburg many times and would know the best places to go and things to do.

The sun broke through and sent the clouds scudding off. Delk got up and washed, then ate the rest of the meat and bread left over from supper. He watered the horses and made sure the gate was securely fastened. Captain Flood's cousin had said their possessions were safe here. Delk threw his blanket over his weapons and took the path past the house and out onto the dirt street.

He wandered along, stopping once to watch slaves making bricks and again to follow surveyors staking out a meadow. Two small boys chased a hog past him and down a ravine. Now through the trees ahead of him he glimpsed a big brick building. He stopped an old man and asked him what it was.

"That double pile?" the old man asked, looking where the boy pointed. "That be the great palace where Governor Spotswood wastes public monies." He shook his head. "A great waste for he never stays in it. He's always gadding abroad. Leaving this very day for the western mountains, I hear." He went off, shaking his head, and muttering something about "a sinful waste."

Delk walked toward the palace. When he got near, he saw servants, both white and black, scurrying in and out of the doors. There were a half-dozen horses there, some saddled, others with packs on their backs. A man hurried past the young ranger with a hammer and plane in his hands. He stopped beside another man holding the lines of two pack horses.

"Where's the governor off to now, Bob?" the man with the plane queried.

"The western mountains," answered the second man. "He's gathering an expedition at Germanna out beyond Fredericksburg. He'll get us all killed yet, you mark my words. Those that don't get killed by Injuns will be et by bears."

The carpenter laughed and shook one of the packs. "You've got along enough wine to cure your sorrows," he said with a wink.

"Fat lot I'll see of it," the servant said sourly. But then he added, "The governor's a gentleman, Sam. He ain't like you and me, he's used to having fine things even when he's journeying about the wilderness."

"Oh, aye, maybe so," said the first man. "Me, I don't care for such airs anyway. I'm content to be an honest carpenter."

"Honest!" cried the servant. "You? You what builds houses out of knotholes and charges two prices for 'em. You're a scoundrel and you know it, Sam Holmes. Git back to your nailing and sawing."

Grinning, the carpenter sauntered off. A coach with six horses clattered around the corner and swept past Delk to the rear of the palace, a handsome coach decorated with bright paint and some kind of insignia on the door. It must surely be the governor's.

A big man appeared suddenly in the doorway of the mansion, a handsome man with imposing carriage. The governor! Delk knew it was. Some day he hoped he could tell his sisters about this. The man stared down the steps at the pack horses, and then a second man appeared behind him, waving a sheaf of papers in the air.

"Excellency," he cried. "Your excellency! What about . . ."

Governor Spotswood turned about impatiently, "Oh, very well," he said and disappeared into the palace again.

Delk waited, thinking to see the governor leave. He would dearly love to make such an expedition himself, but not with the governor. All that finery was too much for Delk's simple tastes. But there were plenty he could find who'd be willing to accompany him maybe sometime. At the fort the traders were forevermore talking about finding a passage through the mountains and about trading with Indians who had never seen a white man before. Or they talked about gold and silver and old maps to lost mines. Oh, it was fine talk and made Delk shiver with excitement. He longed to go way off to the western reaches of Virginia, not to find gold or riches but just to see, to know what was there beyond the blue hills and deep in the forests.

Someone touched him on the arm and Delk turned. It was a sailor, tanned and weathered and pigtailed. He was red eyed and unshaved and smelled strongly of ale. "Which way to the docks, mate?" he asked hoarsely.

"I . . . I don't reckon there are any hereabouts," answered Delk.

The sailor swayed back and forth. "Wotcher mean, no docks," he bawled. "Where's the water? Where's the ships?"

"You've missed 'em by a matter of miles," one of the pack horse men called out. "Better try again."

"What . . . what day be it?" asked the sailor blinking in astonishment at the men and animals around him.

"August twentieth," Servant Bob told him. "And in case all that drink has made you forget the year, 'tis 1716."

"The twentieth!" cried the sailor. "Then me ship's sailed. Me ship's gone. All me mates has left me behind," and he looked as though he might weep at this sad thought. After a minute he hoisted up his trousers jauntily and said, "Glory, what a piece of good luck."

He stumbled away and went weaving back and forth across the palace green toward the main street. Everyone laughed delightedly.

The morning was getting along and Delk made up his mind not to wait to see the governor depart. That might be hours yet. Anyway he'd just wanted a glimpse of the man who had built Fort Christanna and of whom so much, both good and bad, was said. He'd had that glimpse and now he was ready to see more of the shops and stores.

He idled about the town the rest of the morning. By noon he found himself at Sue Allen's Ordinary and there the tipsy sailor turned up again. The seaman had started in the door, but was met by a man who said firmly, "Not in here. You ain't fit. And I happen to know you ain't got a penny in your pocket."

The sailor good naturedly turned away, but since several men were passing by, headed for the back of the ordinary, the sailor joined them, as though he thought he might have better luck at the back door. Delk tagged along too for he could see that something of interest was going on in the rear.

The yard was crowded and in the center of the crowd stood Captain Captain. He had fastened a small, wooden shingle to a tree trunk to shoot at. For pennies the Indian would shoot at the mark with his bow and arrow, or allow anyone who wanted to pay to try his hand with the weapons. The sailor shoved his way into the mob, but Delk remained at the outer edge.

A well-dressed man picked up a yellow leaf and went and stuck it on the target. It was half the size of the shingle. "For a shilling, hit that three times in a row!" he challenged.

The Saponi's face didn't change a wink. He simply raised the bow and three times sent an arrow into the little leaf. The white man shook his head admiringly and handed over the shilling.

"I can do that," boasted the sailor. "I can hit a hair on a captain's nose at a hundred faces—a hundred p-paces. Gimme the bow. I can shoot, gimme the bow."

"Let him try," cried one of the spectators. "I'll pay," and he handed over his money.

The sailor took the bow and after much slipping and fumbling notched the arrow. "Now lemme 'lone," he commanded, "I can do it." He raised the bow and aimed directly at the man who had paid his fee.

"Look out!" yelled the spectator, throwing up his arms. The chief grabbed the seaman by the shoulder and turned him toward the tree with the shingle.

"You wasn't in no danger," someone assured the man who had been aimed at. "I'll wager he can't hit his own big toe."

The sailor, swaying slowly on his feet, snatched and jerked at the string and finally the arrow left the bow, wobbling as though it too had had more ale than was good for it. It rose sharply upward and then wavered down onto the roof of a stable. A small boy went scrambling up to retrieve it.

"Fine shot! Oh, well done," bawled somebody in the crowd, and amid great laughter the seaman went shambling off.

Now several more men pushed up to try their hands, but Captain Captain shook his head. He gathered up his arrows and stuck them and the bow in his quiver and left the yard. As he passed Delk, he beckoned, and the boy was glad to go with the chief, happy for his company. As they walked along the street, the chief turned his earnings over in his hand, counting and recounting the shillings and pence. At last he seemed satisfied.

They stopped at a store, where the Saponi bought a bag full of barley sugar sticks and gave two of these to Delk, two lengths of fiery-red ribbon, and a pair of scissors. He drew out a leather thong and strung the scissors on it by one of the handles and then tied it around his neck.

Strolling down the streets of Williamsburg, he looked very odd indeed, with the ribbon threaded through the lobes of his ears, the scissors dangling from his neck, and a stick of barley sugar protruding from his mouth. Delk could hardly keep from grinning.

Yet at the same time he had a warm feeling of respect for the chief, who had managed his prisoner so wisely and knew how to get along in the woods as well as anyone possibly could. But he hadn't been at a loss in the white man's town either. Without exerting himself he'd earned enough money to buy things he'd evidently wanted for some time. If he ever got a chance to come back to Williamsburg, he'd be glad to have Captain Captain along.

"Amen!" said the Chief, glancing at his reflection in a window glass.

Sitting in the warm grass near the powder magazine, Delk felt mighty pleased with himself. The prisoner had been put safely in

gaol. And Delk hadn't lost or left behind a single thing, not his pistols or his cap or a saddlebag or anything. He had not left a gate open or a saddle girth undone or any of the other half-a-hundred foolish unthinking things he was accustomed to doing. So all was well with him.

"Maybe I'm improving," he thought.

Now he and Captain Captain were ready and waiting for the commander. It was midafternoon and still Captain Flood hadn't appeared. The horses cropped the grass contentedly. Captain Captain sat cross-legged on the ground, motionless and unsmiling. People passed and Delk watched them. One was the drunken sailor, sober now and looking tired and ill. A woman pushed a barrow of oyster shells along the road. Two men crossed the green, carrying a load of scantlings on their shoulders. They went slowly and the planks bounced smoothly between them.

The sun was warm and the grass pleasantly soft. Delk was almost asleep when Captain Flood suddenly appeared beside him, leading his horse and accompanied by a small man with a flopping black hat. For a minute Delk thought he was dreaming. It was the horse thief!

"Rogers, this here's Jamie Pigg, a new ranger," said Flood briefly. "I'll be back in a spell." He flung his reins to the tiny man and rushed into the brick magazine.

Jamie Pigg swept off his hat revealing a head of the brightest red hair Delk had ever seen. The little man grinned at the boy. "Oh, aye, 'tis me, lad," he said softly. "Sorry about what happened last night. I 'opes the lady didn't harm you none. I hid and seen what 'appen. I made to come back and tell her she was mistook, but I seen she was in no mood to listen. So I stayed snug."

Delk rubbed the place where the riding whip had struck. They hadn't been hard blows, but they had stung and, worse yet, humiliated.

"Thanks for your help," he said bitterly.

"Ah, now, I've said I was sorry," soothed Pigg. "We'll be fine chums now and we'd ought to get on together. What's your name?"

"It ain't horse thief, anyhow," said Delk angrily.

Jamie Pigg looked astonished. "Now you don't think I was trying to steal the lady's 'orse," he cried. "I was a-loosening the bit. She 'ad it too tight. Nothing ruins a 'orse's mouth as quick as that. One thing I know about is 'orses and I can't abide to see a fine one mistreated. Captain Flood's got 'is a mite too tight too."

He reached up and carefully loosened the cheek strap. Delk didn't know whether he was telling the truth or not, but there was little he could do but believe the little man. Certainly the commander's bit was cutting into the corner of the animal's mouth.

"At home I called myself a jockey," said Jamie Pigg. "I'm the right size for it, you see, just under nine stone. But I wasn't what you might term the best one ever, 'ardly never won a race. So I come to America to find work with some gentleman in 'is stables. But the place ain't to my liking; folks be rude and uncivil, and gentlemen are piteous scarce. So I signed up with your captain till December. I can put me wages by, don't you see, to pay me passage back to London, and oh, aye, it'll be a great day when I see the place again." He sighed sadly.

Delk stood up. He was a head taller than the little man and could look straight down at that coppery hair. All of a sudden it occurred to him that he was no longer the newest recruit, that Jamie Pigg was a ranger greener and more ignorant than he was.

With that red hair, short stature, and strange way of talking— well, Jamie Pigg was in for a hard time! Grinning to himself, Delk planned the misery he was going to inflict on the newcomer.

# Chapter 6

# *"The powder!"*

The rest and good feeding in Captain Flood's cousin's meadow had made the pack horses frisky and hard to manage. Delk walked beside them and he and Captain Captain talked sweetly and softly to them, but every now and then they had to throw in a good hard thwack.

However it was not until they were half a dozen miles south of the James River ferry that the animals grew less frolicsome and settled down to a steady gait carrying the wallets of powder. Then Delk fell back to walk beside the jockey on Nuck. Since they had left Williamsburg, Captain Flood had been talking steadily to Jamie Pigg. At last he had said all he had to say apparently and had dropped behind the others, riding slowly along with his reins loose over the pommel. Delk figured he wanted to keep as close to Williamsburg as he could.

"If you're wanting to ride, I'll dismount," offered Jamie.

Delk shook his head. He was enjoying stretching his legs a little and breathing honest air and having the trees and bushes crowd up close around him instead of stores and big houses. Williamsburg was all right to visit and he'd been glad to see it, but he wasn't the kind to live in the limits of a town. He liked the woods, and the more he saw of them the better he liked them.

"No," he added. "You ride, if you're a mind to. Anyhow I doubt

Nuck's noticed he's carrying you, you're such a little mite of a body. We could both ride together and he wouldn't be overburdened."

Jamie Pigg looked relieved. "Well, I 'oped to ride as much as I could," he confessed. "Me boots—they ain't proper for walking in this kind of territory."

Delk glanced at his boots which were much too daintily made for wilderness wear and paper thin besides. "You'll have to get you some new ones," he said. "That ain't the kind of footgear for a ranger, I can tell you."

Jamie frowned. "What does a ranger do?" he asked at last. "The commander—'e made it sound something fine and exciting like it was 'orse racing. But now it don't seem like 'e ever did say what I was to do and all. And I ain't certain he said this here fort was such a long way out in the sticks."

He cast an anxious glance in among the pines, back to where the forest deepened and darkened. Delk wondered what Jamie would think when the trail went into real woods, among the huge beech and oak trees and the thick vines.

"I figured that's what he was telling you, when he was jawing away at you after we left town," said Delk, surprised.

"Not 'im," Jamie answered in disgust. " 'E told me what a fine dancer 'e was and 'ow the ladies loved him and 'ow he was wearing the rufflediest shirt at the ball last night. But never a word about rangers."

Delk grinned, first, because he might have known the commander had to tell about that ball or bust wide open; and secondly, because he might have known Captain Flood would be too fearful this new recruit would run off if he told him the truth about a ranger's duties and way of living. Anybody could tell Jamie was a townsman and not fit for a ranger's life. If the captain hadn't been desperate, he would never have hired this wee little body who didn't know a thimbleful about hunting and scouting.

"For all that, if he hadn't been desperate, he'd never have hired me either," Delk thought, but it gave him some comfort to know that he at least wasn't scared of the woods.

"I reckon you see 'eaps of wild beasts," said Jamie after a while.

"Deer and turkey, if we're lucky," Delk answered. "But when we range we take along dried beef and mess biscuits in our saddlebags, just in case. Mostly though there's always something to eat handy and easily shot, rabbits or goose or something."

The jockey looked amazed. "I wasn't thinking about eating," he said at last. "What I meant was, ain't there wolves and bears and terrible things like that? Don't you often get attacked?"

Delk could hardly keep from laughing, but he managed to keep a straight face. "Oh, well, wolves and bears—a body just has to put up with 'em," he answered carelessly. "In the daytime we keep a sharp lookout and at night we keep a watch. Still, only last week a wolf chewed off a ranger's toes. It was his own fault—he was sleeping and not watching as he should of been. And early in the summer a bear ran off with a little Injun boy no bigger than you, picked him up in his arms and ran." Delk shook his head. "We never seen the boy again."

Jamie turned pale green. "And snakes?" he asked fearfully. "I'm dreadful feared of rattlesnakes, I am. Do you see a great lot of 'em?"

"Well, now," replied Delk, thinking he had never laid eyes on such a scary, lily-livered man, "we do run into rattlers. For that's one of a ranger's duties, you know. We have to go through the wilderness searching the mean critters out, and when we find 'em, we grab 'em up and tie knots in them. That's so they can't escape into any holes when we take them back to the fort. They're right useful, you know. The big ones serve for tying up prisoners and the Injun women braid up the little ones and make blankets out of them for the rangers to sleep under—the recruits, I mean. It makes 'em tough."

Jamie Pigg gave him a sour look. "Pugh! No call to be funny," he said and rode on in silence. But Delk noticed how he kept glancing around uneasily, as though he expected wolves and snakes to come charging out of the undergrowth and get him.

They came to a stream which the horses had to swim. At this time of the year most creeks and even the rivers were so low they could be forded easily. But not this one. Delk mounted in front of the jockey and Nuck waded into the river slowly, going forward without urging while the muddy water rose along his sides till it lifted him gently off his feet.

Jamie Pigg clutched Delk around the waist. "What'd 'e do if a alligator comes long?" he asked squeakily. "Can a 'orse fight off a alligator?"

Delk once again had all he could do to keep from laughing. Alligators? In Virginia? Oh, Jamie Pigg was an ignoramus!

"Ranger horses are specially trained to smell alligators," Delk told him. "They won't go in the water if there's an alligator close by."

Pigg seemed to believe this, and he relaxed a little.

"They don't often make a mistake, just once in a while," Delk added hastily, not wanting Pigg to be too easy. "And there's some alligators just don't seem to have any scent. If one of them comes along—well, it's a bad day."

Once more the jockey tightened his grip on his companion. Delk grinned as he could feel the little man draw up his knees and try to hold his feet out of the water.

They crossed the river without meeting an alligator and rode on. Shadows were lengthening, and though Delk well knew there were several plantations within an hour's ride of here, he could see that the big trees and thick bushes and forest stillness might make a townsman feel as though he had reached the very end of the world, a place where no man had ever been before. The woods were dense and dark and getting darker.

Jamie Pigg sat white-faced and tight-lipped, glancing first one way and then another. When a hawk swooped down across the trail, he cried out and Captain Captain later said scornfully to Delk, "Him mouse. Scared hawk carry him off."

They traveled on. "We're lost ain't we?" asked Jamie Pigg at last.

"Lost?" repeated Delk. "With the trail lying in front of us plain as day?"

Pigg peered ahead of them puzzled. Delk realized suddenly that the things that made the way apparent to him, Captain Flood, and the Indian—the worn places on the forest floor, the blazes almost healed again, the various landmarks—must be invisible to the

Englishman. He remembered several times ranging with the Saponi and being amazed that they were following a trail, a path he couldn't discover no matter how hard he tried. So now he had a sudden feeling of sympathy for the jockey.

"Don't worry," Delk assured him. "We ain't lost nor likely to get lost." But how was this little witless man ever going to make a ranger? Oh, well, it wasn't his worry.

The sun had almost set when they rode out of the woods onto a meadow beside a creek. Captain Flood said he had camped here before and Delk could see it was a good place, moss to sleep on, fallen wood for fires, cane along the creek for the horses, and a spring of cold fresh water at the edge of the meadow.

Delk dismounted and Jamie Pigg slid down after him. Just as his foot touched the ground a big grasshopper flew up out of the weeds with a whirr of wings. In an instant Jamie was back on the horse. "Rattlesnake!" he gasped. "It almost bit me!"

Delk laughed till he almost fell down and had to hold on to Nuck's mane to keep himself upright. But even after he captured the grasshopper in his hand and showed it to Jamie, the little man wouldn't come down off the horse. He sat there while the chief and Delk gathered firewood and set it blazing. At last Jamie got down and came over to the fire, seeming to suppose he would be safe there.

When the powder bags were unloaded and the packsaddles removed, it was discovered that one of the horses had cast a shoe. Captain Flood was delighted.

"There's a plantation less than an hour's ride from here," he announced. "I can have the beast shod there, they've a blacksmith. Captain Captain can go with me to bring the horse back here and I'll join you in the morning."

He beamed. Delk could see he was delighted to get away from them and have the opportunity to tell his adventures in Williamsburg to a new audience.

When the others had gone, Delk and the Englishman sat staring at each other. Deep in the woods a turkey gobbled a good night. "Listen at that," cried Delk. "A monstrous great rattler for sure."

Jamie Pigg grinned a weak grin. "No, it ain't," he answered.

"'Twas a turkey. Gentleman I worked for once had a flock of them in with 'is fowls, fine looking things they were, too." He sighed. "Oh, if I'd known 'ow well off I was with that gentleman."

Lightning bugs gathered along the creek bank, winking off and on in the gloaming like cats' eyes. Delk pointed them out to Jamie and he nodded. "I reckon they've got a powerful sting," he said wretchedly, "like all your flying bugs." He slapped at the side of his head.

Delk baked ash bread on a hot stone and this with dried venison made their supper. For himself he made a tea of sassafras and mints, things his sisters had often made him gather for them to brew. The smell of the steaming tea almost made him homesick. He remembered how they served the tea in their mother's flowered china cups and tried to pretend it was real tea, from the Far East. And how they chattered and put on airs and made him mind his manners. Wouldn't they be horrified to see him squatting here drinking this stuff out of a battered pewter mug, surrounded by the night and the forest, wearing his old deerskin breeches and sleeveless jacket, dirty and worn after a day's travel.

The little Englishman stared off miserably into the trees as though he too were remembering home and missing it sadly.

"Have some tea," offered Delk, feeling a little sorry for him again.

Pigg shook his head. "It might be poison," he said.

Delk was surprised. "I'm drinking it and it ain't hurt me," he pointed out.

"You was born in the Colonies," replied Pigg. "I reckon it might do a Henglishman some real 'arm, not being used to it."

So he drank the spring water but wouldn't touch the tea.

Delk threw some more wood on the fire. The flames sprang up and the light fell on the smooth, gray trunk of a big beech tree. Suddenly Delk was moved to burn his initials in the sleek bark, the way the rangers always did on patrol.

He reached out and grabbed a branch, glowing at one end, out of the fire. But he miscalculated and grabbed too close to the burning end. The wood was hot as Tophet and he flung the stick from him, with a yell, and stuffed his fingers in his mouth.

Jamie Pigg screamed, "Rogers, the powder!"

# Chapter 7

# The return to Fort Christanna

D elk looked wildly around. He had forgotten where the powder was. He couldn't think what could be the matter with it to make Jamie Pigg scream like that.

Then he saw the bags of powder, not a wink away with the smoldering stick he had just flung aside across two of them. He could smell the scorching leather and see it beginning to crisp and curl as the stick burned. In a minute the powder would ignite.

Delk had once seen the explosion and fire caused by a much smaller amount of powder flaming up, less than half of what was in one of those wallets, and he knew well enough that he would never live through it if the bags caught fire.

But somehow he couldn't move. It was only a few seconds that he stood there stock still, his mouth hanging open and his legs frozen stiff, yet it seemed forever. Then Jamie Pigg sprang past him, kicked the stick aside, turned the bags over so that the charred leather was buried against the dirt, and dragged them away from the others.

Delk just stood there still, he hadn't moved an inch. But finally he went to the stream and fetched water in his cap and drenched the scorched places on the bags to make sure no spark was left alive.

Jamie Pigg shook his head. "Blimey!" he said. "That was close, that was. It ain't clever to throw a brand down and not look where it lands."

Delk was silent, staring down at the blisters on his hand. Once again his carelessness had gotten him into trouble. This time it might have been his very last trouble, but for Jamie.

"You saved my life," he muttered finally. "Thank you."

"Reckon I saved mine too," Jamie answered shortly, and nothing more was said on the subject. But after Delk had stretched out on his blanket, he lay for a long time watching the fire burning lower and then flaring up, while he wondered if he was ever going to get over being such a woodenhead.

The light from the dying blaze shimmered on the leaves overhead. The katydids creaked and an owl hooted, "Hoo, hoo, hoo, hoo-awww!" in a deep, wild voice. In the flickering shadows Pigg too was awake. Delk could see his head turning this way and that, and his eyes gleaming as he strained to see and hear the many enemies creeping up on him through the dark. When Captain Captain stalked into the camp from the woods, the little jockey sprang up from his blanket and settled himself with his back to a log, prepared to stay awake all night, Delk supposed.

Captain Captain did not even glance at them but rolled himself into his blanket and was soon snoring busily. The sound made Delk suddenly drowsy and he turned on his side and shut his eyes. "But ain't it funny?" he thought just before he fell asleep, "that little feller, so scared to death of everything out here in the woods, he was the one that risked his life to save me and the powder and didn't seem to think it was a brave thing at all."

The rangers had finished their evening meal when Delk and the others arrived at Fort Christanna the next day. Captain Flood took Jamie Pigg to the mess hall while Delk was to unload the powder. "Stryker will give you the key to the powder room," the commander told him. "He's at headquarters, I reckon, or should be."

Stryker had been in charge while Captain Flood was away and Delk had a feeling he had enjoyed it. No doubt he would still be at headquarters hoping the commander was going to stay away another day or so. And sure enough there he sat writing at the captain's table. He looked up and grunted when Delk came in and then turned back to his work. Delk asked for the key and Stryker handed it over with one hand, while he sprinkled sand over the ink with the other.

"Right side of the magazine," he said shortly and, dipping his quill into the ink, returned to his letter.

Overhead the sky was still pale with summer light but inside the palisade dark had already come. The blacksmith's forge made a dull-red glow, and here and there one of the buildings was lit up and light streamed out through the open doors.

Delk passed the schoolhouse where the Indian children came to hear their letters and there sat the Reverend Charles Griffin, bent over a book while a single candle flickered beside him. From the Indian company's headquarters there were shouts of laughter and then an angry voice bellowed something that was drowned in song. Some traders must have arrived from a long stay in the wilderness and were celebrating their safe return.

Delk grinned to himself. Oh, he was glad he'd left home. What did life on the farm have to offer to compare with this—all this color and excitement and the thrill of knowing he was helping to build something new and strong and wonderful? He tried to think gravely for a minute of the rangers' responsibilities to the farmers and towns-men of Virginia, the part they had to play in keeping things safe and peaceful.

But in his heart he knew that what really pleased him was the thought of all the wild, unknown, marvelous country to the west and that with the other rangers he was helping to assure the day when it would be opened up and explored. And oh, Lordee, he did hope he was one of the ones to do the exploring.

The magazine was a double-walled log house near the Indian company's trading store. One half was used by the trading company and the other half by the rangers. Delk wished for a minute he'd brought a lantern. Just as well not, though, he told himself. He wouldn't want to do something careless and blow up the whole fort. Better let fire in any form alone.

The door unlocked easily, and he turned back toward the horses. One of them suddenly whinnied and reared sharply. The packsaddle and the wallets of powder slid to the ground.

Delk rushed forward to keep any of the animals from treading on the bags and breaking them open. A figure loomed up out of the dark and he jumped. It was William Stryker.

"Having trouble, Rogers?" he asked.

"Horse's furniture broke loose," answered Delk. "I reckon he's tired and hungry like me, to act up so." Or else he didn't like you sneaking up in the dark, he added to himself.

"Trouble's one thing you never seem to have to do without, ain't it?" Stryker pointed out sourly. "Here, I'll hold the horses and you get the powder inside."

Delk made a face in the dark. He wished it was somebody else who had come along to lend him a hand.

He worked carefully, unloading the bags one by one, for he was determined that he wasn't going to make a dumb mistake with Stryker looking on. None of the wallets the horse had dropped had split, which was a blessing.

He deposited the last of the powder and locked the door. Stryker held out his hand and Delk put the key in it. "Never expected to see you alive again," the man said slyly. "Thought sure that Seneca would find a chance to slip a knife in your ribs."

"Well, he didn't," Delk replied shortly. "We didn't have any trouble with him."

"Maybe he's just biding his time," said Stryker, and walked away.

Now what did he mean by that, Delk wondered, as he lead the horses toward the horse pen. Come to think of it, what would happen to the Seneca at Williamsburg? Would they just question him and let him go? Was he perhaps turned loose and right this minute coming back to Fort Christanna to avenge his honor? Delk didn't see any need for Stryker to bring the thing up at all.

He fed and rubbed down the horses quickly for he was eager for his own supper and bed. On the way to the mess hall he stopped at the powder magazine and checked to make sure that he had locked the door and left all in order. For as unthinking as he was, it was best to make assurance doubly sure.

In the mess hall there was one old Indian woman kneeling beside a pot on the big stone hearth. Delk's supper of meat and bread and a bowl of cider sat on the table. He ate it all and wished for some more. He must have looked hungry, for the woman suddenly fetched another loaf of bread from the bin, set it down beside him, and re-filled his cider bowl.

"Thanky," muttered Delk shyly. He had learned to get along with the men, but these dark-skinned women still made him uncomfortable and uneasy.

When he was through eating, he left the mess room and went into the other side of the building, which served as a barracks. Hurdly was there, working on his pistol by the light of two candles.

"If we had a blacksmith worth shooting, he'd know how to file a pistol lock," he muttered and then looked up and winked at Delk.

"A heap of folks at Williamsburg said tell you hello, they ain't heard a real lie since last time you came to see 'em," Delk told him.

Hurdly grinned. "Well, it's certain sure when I go to town I know how to do something besides catch butterflies," he answered. "But you and Captain Flood . . . " he broke off, shaking his head. "That butterfly you brung back with you, he's the biggest I ever seen."

Delk shrugged. "I reckon Captain Flood must have been famously anxious to have a full troop of rangers, to bring Jamie Pigg back here to make the twelfth man," he admitted. "He don't know a pin's worth about hunting or scouting and he's scared to death of gnats, Indians, trees—most nigh everything."

Hurdly grunted. "The commander's wanted a full troop for a long time now—twelve names to look good on the report he has to fill out," he said.

He filed a moment, then looked up again. "Reckon that's one name he'll wish he could cross off, if trouble comes along. 'Course, we've done little enough fighting these past two years, but here we be ready to fight when the time comes."

"I wish we'd do less manure hauling and gun cleaning and more fighting," Delk said. "I reckon Pigg can do these tasks like the rest of us, but somebody'll have to go along with him on patrol and hold his hand." He paused, then added thoughtfully, "Maybe he won't have to range. He sure can't ride out without no horse nor weapons. He ain't got but the clothes on his back."

"There's extra horses in the pen, some of the Indian company's," Hurdly pointed out, "and Captain Flood can get any of them he needs. Weapons too," he nodded.

Delk hadn't known that. He thought each ranger could sign up only if he brought his own horse and equipment. The commander was a body to reckon with, the boy could see that. He wondered how it'd be to order folks around and do pretty much what you wanted to do, like Captain Flood? Well, it was a thing he'd likely never have to worry about.

"Then Pigg could stay, if he don't die of fright," Delk mused.

Hurdly chuckled. "He won't last till December," he predicted. "Nor you neither, young feller-me-lad. Chances are you'll git out of bed some morning and leave your head lying there and the cooks will throw it in the pot with the rest of the turnips."

He snapped his pistol lock shut and stuck the weapon in his belt and left the barracks. Delk yawned. Talking of bed reminded him of how sleepy he was. He debated whether he should go looking for Pigg. The little Englishman should get some sleep too, for, from the look in Hurdly's eye, he was going to have a rough time for the next few days! But he was much too tired to do more than fall on his bed.

As a matter of fact, Delk figured Jamie would have suffered enough from his own fears and alarms without any help from the rangers. He jumped and turned pale at every strange sound, he never went to bed without inspecting the straw mattress and the blanket for venomous creatures. Every morning he went to the door and opened it cautiously and rolled a blue eye round and about to make sure the yard was clear of bears and wolves before he went out.

In spite of his precautions snakes and spiders got into his bedding and his boots and even into his mug of ale at supper one night. It was easy enough to tease the little man, and the rangers held their sides when he screamed like a girl over the toad in his drink or slept for three nights running on top of a table after he'd found a puffing adder in his bed.

Delk couldn't help feeling sorry for him. After all, it was hardly Pigg's fault that he'd been raised in London and never been near a wilderness till he was a grown man. Nor was it his fault he was so little and ugly. Delk wished he could think of some way to help the jockey, to make him realize that there was no need to be so scared.

The other men would like him then, Delk was certain. For Jamie was marvelous with horses, even the balkiest would do what he wanted it to, and the nerviest ones calmed down and became easy when he spoke to them. He was so watchful and easily alarmed, he ought to be fine out on patrol, thought Delk with a grin. He could probably hear Indians coming thirty miles off and smell gunpowder even farther.

One night early in September, Delk was lying on his bed when Hurdly came in from guard duty.

"Now that poor little feller, that there Henglishman," he said suddenly. "What he needs is some new footgear, ain't that right? Why, them boots is so full of holes snakes could crawl in 'em while he was just walking through the weeds. Ain't that right?"

He grinned at Delk, who didn't answer, since it was hardly a secret about Jamie's boots. The jockey complained all the time about them and begged his barrack companions to find him new ones.

"What we got to do, you and me," Hurdly went on, taking off his equipment and placing it on the bed, "is fetch that runty little feller over to the Saponi village and get him some Injun shoes, a good pair of moccasins. A real good pair."

He chuckled and Delk knew the chuckle boded no good for Jamie Pigg. "How come you want to play such mean tricks on Pigg?" he asked. "He can't help it he's so homely and little."

Hurdly looked surprised. "It ain't on account of he's little and ugly enough to sour milk," he answered. "It's on account of he's such a coward. Anyway, I seen you laughing fit to bust this morning when Crowder yelled there was a mad wolf behind him and growled and he clumb right up the wall."

Delk grinned. It had been funny. But there'd been enough of it. Maybe he ought to warn Jamie that Hurdly meant to play some kind of trick on him at the Saponi village. Not that it would do any good, Jamie was so edgy all you had to do was say "boo!" at him to make him jump a mile.

Just then John Tupper leaned in the door of the barracks. "Rogers," he called, "Captain wants to see you. And you better take a tight grip on your skin, for he means to have it off. I ain't never seen him so mad!"

# Chapter 8

# "Gone to the wracks"

*D*elk propped himself up on his elbows and stared at Tupper in bewilderment. "What'd I do now?" he asked despairingly.

Tupper shrugged. "He ain't said what it was, but it must have been something terrible. He's so mad he was most nigh spitting fire and brimstone."

Hurdly slapped Delk on the shoulder. "I told you you wasn't going to last till December," he pointed out and guffawed. "Reckon they'll be proud to see you back home."

Delk stood up. He wouldn't go back home, that was certain. He just wouldn't. He didn't care what.

"Best not tarry," said Tupper. "The captain's got no humor for waiting."

Delk snatched up his cap and hurried out into the night. It was cool, there was already more than a hint of fall in the night air, a smell of dry leaves and fires and dust. The katydids had slowed their song and crickets called here and there. Delk glanced up and the stars gleamed fuzzily in a hazy sky.

What had he done? The days since his return from Williamsburg had passed quickly. The commander had had a touch of ague and the troop had done little more than routine work around the fort, spending most of the hot weather in the river or fishing along the banks. If Delk had made any more blunders or forgotten anything important, he'd have heard about it before now. What could it be?

Oh, why in the world couldn't he learn to keep his head and make certain he did all his tasks properly?

In his room Captain Flood was standing by the hearth and Delk thought he did, for a fact, look angry enough to set the logs ablaze just by glancing at them. He seemed three times his normal size, his face was red, and his eyes bulged and flashed.

Delk quailed in his boots. When the commander roared around the fort yard, telling the rangers what to do, he seemed cocky and pompous, and though Delk didn't like being trounced by the captain for forgetting his cap or neglecting to curry a horse, he'd never been really scared of him before. But this time Nicholas Flood frightened him in truth. Whatever he'd done it must be something fearful.

"Rogers!" said the captain in a strangled voice. "Rogers!"

He didn't seem able to go on, and Delk waited, half-prepared to run out the open door if the commander charged toward him.

"I ought to have you flogged," Flood burst out at last. "If it was in my power, I'd have you drawn and quartered. I can't believe it, a ranger to behave so . . ."

Oh, what in heaven's name had he done? Delk's mind raced over the past days. He'd been on time for everything, he'd checked everything he'd done several times to make doubly sure he'd not forgotten anything. He had concentrated so hard on all his tasks he'd chewed his lower lip half off.

"I trusted you," went on the captain. "I knew you were young and careless and unthinking, but I was willing to give you a chance. I was willing to give you occasion to prove you had the makings of a man. And now this . . . "

He sputtered for a while. "I should have done it when we got back from Williamsburg, but I trusted you," he groaned. "Today I got up off a sick bed to go to the powder room and tally up the wallets and issue fresh powder . . . and if I hadn't checked, there'd not have been one left in another day or so, I'll lay that. Every ounce of powder'd have been stolen!"

Delk's mouth dropped open in astonishment. "Sir," he finally managed to say, "sir, I ain't been near the magazine since I stored the powder when we got back from the capital."

"That's what I'm saying!" bellowed Captain Flood. "You left the

powder room unlocked on purpose. And now you and your helpers have made off with half the powder! Where have you hid it?"

Delk wondered if this was another trick and if the commander had decided to join in the fun of teasing him. Captain Flood reached out and grabbed the boy's shirt and knotted it in his fist. "Where? Where?" he snarled.

Delk swallowed. It was no trick, this was something real and he was in grave trouble. "I . . . sir, I ain't no thief," he cried at last, growing angry himself. "I never stole, not so much as a ball of lead. And I ain't got no helper. How could I have?—I never left the magazine unlocked. You can ask Stryker, he was there. He saw me lock the place and I gave him the key."

The commander stared at him silently for several minutes. Then with a half-shake he turned him loose and strode to the door and bawled, "Stryker!" in a voice like Judgment Day.

Stryker lived in the other half of the building but he took his time getting there. He came into headquarters with his slouching arrogant walk and stood just inside the door. "Wanted me?" he asked.

Captain Flood made a great effort to calm himself and hold his voice down. "Stryker, was you with Rogers the night he put up the powder? You never mentioned it. Did you see him lock the powder room?"

Stryker rubbed his cheek with the back of his hand and Delk could hear the harsh scrape of his whiskers in the quiet. "I was by there," he said with a curt nod. "Boy was having trouble with the horses and I held 'em. In the dark he *looked* to be locking the place up, but I didn't check to see. Never thought about it. Figured any ranger to do his duty."

"I *did* lock it," Delk exclaimed hotly. "I did lock the door. And I never stole nothing. What would I want with powder? And I ain't helping nobody steal. I ain't. It's the truth!"

Stryker and the captain looked at him for a long time, and Delk could see that neither one believed him. Delk thought he ought to say something more, but what could he say now that would possibly help him? He was almost too shocked to think clearly.

That night he was unloading the powder—had there been something strange about that horse acting up as it did? Or was it just natural horse meanness? He didn't know, he didn't know! Stryker being Billy-on-the-spot, to hold the beasts and watch the business of putting the powder away—was there something suspicious about that? You could tell Flood trusted Stryker. Even if he had been up to some deviltry, Flood wouldn't believe it. Not on Delk Rogers' word.

"The powder's gone, Rogers," the Captain said, "and it's a fact you was the last person in the magazine. Your carelessness has cost the colony money it could ill spare. It has disgraced the rangers. This'll make folks think ill of the very men they should most trust."

He frowned and Delk wondered if the commander was thinking that this incident might mean he wouldn't be so welcome at balls and dinner parties at Williamsburg and the plantations around and about. Delk wished that was all he had to worry about. His whole future was at stake here. Would he be locked up or given thirty-nine lashes across the back? Or dismissed from the rangers?

"Less than three months and I'll be done with the rangers," Flood went on. "And I wanted to leave a record behind me that I'd be proud of, one that had no blemish whatsoever. And now . . . now . . . the powder will be sold to the Injuns and used against us. The powder that was in *my* keeping, *my* powder!"

He thumped his fist on the table and gritted his teeth in rage. Then he slumped and the boy thought he would surely faint dead away. Stryker took him by the arm. The commander straightened up and his head turned toward Delk. There was fear in his eyes, the stark fear of an Indian uprising along the whole length of the tomahawk border.

Delk turned suddenly cold. It might happen he'd be considered the traitor who stole the powder and sold it to the Indians to start their war. Oh, he was sure to be hanged now. Flood would have no mercy on him. He was doomed. There was no longer any need to worry about his future. It would be settled by a noose.

"Don't leave the fort, Rogers," the captain ordered. "I'll decide what to do about you later."

He waved his hand and Delk turned and left the room. Stryker did not follow him. Glancing back, he saw the commander and his right-hand man huddled together around the table talking intently. He went on. He had never been so heavyhearted.

How could he have failed to lock the magazine? He knew he had. He remembered the whole thing, the summer night and how tired he'd been and even the thack! the wallets had made when they hit the ground beside the rearing horse. That Stryker, what was he doing sneaking up like that? Delk recalled that Stryker's presence had forced him to be extra careful. He was positive he'd locked that door, positive that he'd even checked it on his way back from the horse pen. Well, almost positive, a thickhead like himself could never be too sure about anything.

One thing he could be sure about right now, though, and that was he'd be gone to the wracks if something wasn't done to save him.

## Chapter 9

# Saponi Town

*T*he next morning, for the first time in his life, Delk couldn't eat breakfast. He had lain awake all night, picturing Delk Rogers tied to a pole with the lash whistling toward his bare back, or Delk Rogers staring hopelessly out of the barred window of a prison, or, worst of all, Delk Rogers mounting the gallows steps toward the waiting noose, disgraced, a traitor.

Now the porridge stuck in his dry throat. He had to help it down with a swallow of cider, and that was all he could manage. He got up from the table and went back to the barracks and sat disconsolately on the edge of his bed.

There was much coming and going in the barracks and all over the fort. Captain Flood had wasted no time. Patrols consisting of one ranger and as many as ten or twelve Indians left the fort to patrol every trail and keep an eye out for any danger signals. Runners were sent to warn the frontier plantations of possible trouble. Flood and Captain Hix of the trading company conferred a dozen times a day, running back and forth between the two men's headquarters, with great fuss and flurry.

No one spoke to Delk. He did not know whether this was because they were all so busy they didn't have time to pay him attention or because they suspected that he was indeed a thief and a traitor. He sat on his bed, staring into space for hours at a time, then he would pace the barracks, thinking what he was to do, and thus that whole day passed.

He wished he had someone to talk to and ask advice of. He thought about Hurdly, but then he recalled that Lane and Stryker had always been friends, and Delk's dark suspicions of Stryker could not be repressed. He told himself this was foolish, for Stryker was obviously Flood's most trusted ranger, and now he was almost as busy as the commander. He gave orders left and right, going at a pace that was almost a hurry for Stryker, who generally took his sweet time about everything.

Anyway, Hurdly was one of the first to be sent on patrol. Delk had no desire to talk to the others. He sat and pondered his problem and wondered what really had happened and whether Stryker was responsible and what would follow. The second morning Stryker, on an inspection tour, spied him and set him to scrubbing the words and pictures scribbled by some of the rangers in their spare time from the barrack walls. He ordered him to chop wood and even mend a floor in one of the buildings. Delk was glad. Working was far better than simply sitting and waiting or pacing worriedly.

Once or twice he thought about running away. He even got as far as collecting all his gear to have it ready to carry off in the night. He wouldn't go home, no never now. Not a failure and a shame. He'd run off to the woods and wait for some trader to come by, headed south into Indian country. A trader would be glad to let him come along, no matter who he was or what he'd done as a ranger, to tend the horses and look after the truck. He'd heard two of the trading company men talking about how hard it was to get pack-horse helpers. No one wanted to hire out to someone else when he could get together some trinkets and strike out as his very own master, trading where he pleased.

But Delk couldn't sneak away like that. Some might think it a confession, he figured. And it was certainly giving up. He gritted his teeth and resolved to stay. If Jamie Pigg could hang on, so could he.

No one had troubled to show Jamie the real business of being a ranger. Still he wasn't idle. The little jockey had been working as hard as the rest. With so much riding in and out the care of the horses had kept him busy, and the strain showed in his face. He staggered into the barracks at night and cried, "Corblimey, I'll never live to see the Thames again," and fell across his bed so still that Delk thought he might actually have died, except that he began to snore.

Once in a while Delk's path crossed that of Captain Flood, and the commander gave the boy a look that chilled his blood. "He'd like to see me hanged here and then taken to Williamsburg and hanged once more for good measure," thought Delk. However, the captain never spoke to him, simply hurried on, for the fort was full of activity. Not just the preparations for a possible Indian uprising, but every other kind of event seemed suddenly to crowd inside the palisades.

A group of Cherokee Indians, tall and proud, with scalp locks about the size of a Spanish dollar on the crown of their heads, came to the fort to secure passports and to hand over their arms to the rangers as the law required before traveling through Virginia. All were in breechclouts but they carried white man's clothes rolled in bundles so they would be clean and dignified for their conference with Governor Spotswood. After eating and drinking and hearing a talk by Captain Flood, the braves left, each with six skins to buy food and lodging in Williamsburg.

Long lines of pack horses came and went through the gate. The warehouse never seemed to close its doors, and the blacksmith banged all night long. Will Crumbly, a ranger, was thrown from his horse and suffered a broken leg. One of the traders accused another of stealing his skins, and a terrible fight ensued back and forth across the yard.

Another day some minor officials of the colony arrived. Two of the cannons were fired as they entered the fort. Then for a while Delk almost forgot his troubles watching and listening to all that went on. Commander Flood and Captain Hix welcomed the newcomers. Standing in a row, several of the scholars from the Indian school repeated the church catechism, sang a hymn, and recited a Psalm in high squeaky voices. They stumbled very little over the English words and Delk marveled. He didn't think he'd ever do so well with the Saponi language.

Then their teacher stuck the head of an axe into a log. The Indian boys stood twenty paces away and shot arrows at the eye of the axe. It was remarkable how few of them missed sending their feathered shafts through the hole; but the officials seemed hardly to care for this entertainment and left soon after, hurrying off with their servants and their horses loaded with baggage.

The days passed slowly. Gradually the fort lost its tension. Delk no longer woke in the night thinking he'd heard the sound of guns and war cries. September went by, one blue day after another; leaves began to turn on the trees, and the nights were crisp.

Fewer patrols went out, and there were more rangers about in the barracks and yard, sleeping, lounging, and gossiping in their old lazy way. If any of them had harbored suspicions of Delk, they no longer showed it, and they treated him the way they formerly had, as one of them. Delk took hope. Only Stryker and the captain continued to be curt with him and give him wary looks.

"Let Stryker cut his eye around at me if he's a mind to," thought Delk. "For I mistrust him a heap more than he mistrusts me. And maybe the day'll come when I'm watching him sharper than he watches me and I'll see him up to some mischief."

One day Delk was cleaning one of the cannon and Captain Flood mounted the platform to stand beside him.

"Rogers," he said heavily.

"Yes, sir," answered Delk.

"Rogers," repeated the captain. He looked tired. The whole episode had sobered him considerably, Delk thought. Some of his proud feathers had dragged in the mud and they weren't going to be the same again. Perhaps it had been a good thing.

"There doesn't seem to be any disturbance on the border," the captain went on abruptly. "It doesn't do to let our guard down, you understand. Trouble might come any moment. But it doesn't seem likely. I'm sorry I doubted your honesty, Rogers. Anyway," he shrugged and seemed not to know just what he meant to say. "Anyway, if you don't learn to take heed, Rogers, you're bound to end up in trouble. Still the fort needs you. You'll be riding out on patrol again soon."

"Yes, sir," repeated Delk and bent to his polishing with vigor. It was suddenly grand to be alive and young, to be a real ranger again.

When the task was done, Delk climbed down from the platform and started for the barracks. He passed the schoolhouse as the children came running out with whoops and shrieks. A game of football began at once. One of the boys dropped a small leather ball and began to kick it ahead of him as he ran. The others scrambled to get it, and soon there was a mass of brown bodies, pushing and shoving. Delk grinned to see them and he wished for a minute that he could join in the fun.

Inside the barracks Jamie Pigg sat trying to mend his boot with some leather from an old glove. He held one up to show Delk. "Time was, it was leather with 'oles 'ere and there," he sighed sadly. "Now it's just 'oles with leather 'ere and there. Enough 'oles in this one boot to make a sieve."

From across the room where he was cutting paper for use as cartridge tubes, Lane called, "You'd ought to go over to Saponi Town and get some moccasins. I've done told you and told you I'd take you any time."

Delk was surprised at this generous offer on Hurdly's part, and then he realized good intentions had little to do with it. Hurdly had planned all along to play some kind of prank on Pigg in the Indian town.

Jamie looked terrified. "No, no," he cried. "I want no part of them red Indians. God's truth, they scare me something dreadful."

"Aw, you should go, Jamie," urged Delk. "You need the moccasins. They're better than boots any day."

The jockey shook his head. "I'll do without," he replied stubbornly. "I don't trust them 'eathen savages. Anyhow, I can't spare the money. I've got to save me money to get 'ome."

"You don't need money," put in Hurdly, winking at Delk. "You got something to trade?"

Jamie shook his head. "Nothing." Delk was already searching through his chest. He found a red linen handkerchief and threw it to Hurdly. "There. That'll pay for them. I don't use it noway."

Jamie went on stitching the patch. "Better go barefoot than take meself among them murdering brutes and all their axes and knives," he said mournfully. "All them little black eyes and the way they stare at you."

"There's nothing to be afraid of," Delk answered. "They're all peaceable folk. Come along, Jamie. I'll go with you. You and me and Hurdly—we won't be in any danger, not three of us together."

The little man looked thoughtfully down at his boots for a second, and then he stood up. He was quite pale. "He really is scared half to death," thought Delk. In spite of his curiosity about what kind of a trick Lane was going to play on the little Englishman, once again Delk felt sorry for him. He wouldn't let it go too far, he made up his mind. There wasn't any sense in tormenting the tiny man to death.

"All right," agreed Jamie shakily. "I'll go." He stowed away his cobbling tools and put on his big black hat. Hurdly was elated; he was all full of grins and nods and winks.

As they went out the door Hurdly grabbed Jamie by one arm and Delk grabbed him by the other. Together they lifted him off the ground. Jamie gave a sudden kick and grew red in the face. "Put me down, put me down," he bawled. Delk let go hastily and even Hurdly looked surprised.

"I got me pride," said Jamie angrily. "It ain't no lark being under sized and ugly and all. But there's some things a body can't stand. And I won't stand it."

Delk had once more a glimpse of Jamie's courage. There was nothing wrong with his heart; he was surely not a coward. It made Delk almost ashamed to take part in the joke. Still he couldn't help wanting to see what Lane was up to, and also he'd never had a good look at the town.

They went out the gate, down the hill, and along the winding path beside the river. Rocks and rapids made the water roar and murmur, but closer to the village the stream deepened into a still green pool. On the other bank turtles sat along a log like so many cooling meat pies.

As they neared the town, they came on several small sugar-loaf-shaped houses, built of cane and plastered with clay.

"What's them?" asked Delk. "Ovens? I tasted some Indian persimmon bread once, and it was good."

Lane grinned. "I reckon you might say them's ovens. But 'tain't bread they bake, 'tis bodies."

"You mean the 'eathens burn their dead?" cried Jamie, and just then a door in one of the buildings swung wide, a naked brave leaped out and dived into the river with a blood-curdling yell. Jamie almost jumped in himself, and Delk was startled.

"You're a couple of ignorant cusses," cried Hurdly. "Don't ye know a sweat house when you see one?" He explained how the Indians heated stones and put them in the little houses. "Man goes in there with them and he sweats barrels," Hurdly went on. "The Injuns believe sweating is a prime remedy, keeps you free of humors and fevers after you cool off in the river."

Jamie shivered. "Water's un'ealthy," he commented. "Reckon they'll all die off soon."

Delk was glad his sisters hadn't heard of this device. They were forever dinging at him about keeping clean. He believed he preferred sitting in a wooden tub while Cato poured water over him, especially in the winter. Even his sisters had to admit that too much winter-bathing was dangerous and caused body infirmities, and he could often miss a bath by looking thoughtful and coughing gently, as though he might be coming down with something.

They turned away from the river toward the village, a great circle of houses lying in a savannah. The houses were joined, each to its neighbor, so that their backs formed a solid outside wall for the town. The roofs were flat and covered with flakes of bark.

As they approached, a man passed them carrying a string of fish, and then a woman with a basket of corn and a pumpkin, and suddenly a band of painted warriors trotted out of the entrance and crossed the meadow with their rifles swinging rhythmically back and forth in their hands.

Jamie watched them nervously. "I 'ope they keep going away," he breathed softly.

The white men moved along a passageway between two houses, one of three into the town, and stood on the bare, hard-packed earth in the center of the village. Before them in the open square was one tree stump which Hurdly said had been left as a speaking stand for the chiefs and elders. It amused Delk that the Indians enjoyed making speeches, just as Captain Flood did, and he was surprised, for all he'd ever heard from them was a short burst of words and a string of grunts.

For a moment the three looked slowly around. There seemed to be every kind of thing going on—old men smoking pipes on skins, women working, children dancing, and warriors preening themselves before mirrors. To Delk it was almost like a fair back home at the county seat. And he was much interested, too, in the variety of items hanging on the front of the many log dwellings, the haunches of meats, the bunches of plants and feathers, the strings of shells, and the woven grass mats. However, what caught the jockey's eye on the wall of the house nearest them was two sloe-eyed babies, strapped to a board hung from pegs.

" 'Eathen!" exclaimed Jamie in a scandalized voice. " 'Anging children on the wall like they was coats!"

"They're hung up to dry," Hurdly explained, "so they can be stored for winter food along with the pumpkins."

Jamie was outraged. "It ain't a thing to joke about," he cried. "These red Indians might really be cannibals, for all you know."

"I'll take my chances," said Lane. "Now you two wait here. I'll fetch the man who makes the best moccasins and gives the best trade."

He went off and though Delk felt it best to keep a sharp eye on Hurdly, he was so busy watching Jamie, he didn't notice which way the big ranger went. Jamie's blue eyes were rolling here and there, as the villagers passed on their various errands. A couple of dogs ran up and sniffed suspiciously at the white men's legs and bristled and growled about them. A number of children gathered to stare and then a fat woman carrying a reed fish creel. She shook it at them and called out something in a fierce voice and Jamie shrank closer to Delk. Several nearly grown boys suddenly ringed them, staring with blank unsmiling faces.

"Oooo, look at them," whispered Jamie. "Where's Lane? 'Ow come 'e don't come back? 'Ow come 'e's left us like this?"

Delk could hardly hide a grin. He moved off a few steps, and the jockey followed as if the two of them had been tied together and couldn't walk any other way. "Poor Jamie," he thought, "maybe I should have warned him Lane aimed to tease him a mite, for I'm certain Hurdly has put the savages up to something."

But surely Jamie hadn't forgotten these were tributary Indians and friendly. Nothing could happen. Hurdly's trick would soon be over and all would be well.

Now from all directions the Saponi were gathering slowly, warriors and naked children, women of all ages, dogs and even a stray bobtailed horse. Jamie glared around at them, doubling up his tiny

fists. Yet still the crowd streamed toward them, quietly pressing in closer and closer. Delk didn't like their looks. There were too many and they were already too close. He shifted, hoping to edge away before it was too late. The crowd shifted with him in a sort of slow dance, making the same moves he and the jockey made.

A low whimper came from Jamie and he seemed to shrivel up and get even smaller. Delk wanted to tell him it was all a trick, not to worry. But suddenly some of Jamie's fear touched Delk. In an instant the peaceful town and the Indians became a threat. He stiffened, surprised and uncertain, bracing himself for he knew not what.

The sun, sliding down the sky, cast shadows that emphasized the dark-shadowed eyes around him, the still, somehow cruel, mouths, the strong, bony noses. The faces coming toward him were like a row of masks, carved into every kind of hateful, wicked grimace. Were these red savages really as friendly as Delk had thought? Here in their own town might they not do what they pleased with intruding white men? Where was Lane? He wished he would hurry back.

As he turned to the jockey to say something to comfort them both, Jamie plunged toward the passageway where they had entered. Immediately a huge brave, almost twice as tall as Jamie, barred the way. The jockey whirled about and ran toward a second exit, but a crowd of women and children stood between him and it. In a panic he dodged this way and that, but always there was someone to obstruct him. He was caught like a rat inside a trap.

A moment ago it might have been funny to Delk, but not now. He was trapped himself, and whatever was happening was no laughing matter. Jamie came running back and clutched Delk's arm, and Delk couldn't help clutching back. And still the ring of faces pressed closer and closer.

A hand reached out and knocked off Pigg's great hat. The sun fell on his hair like a match on dry timber. His head seemed to blaze and flame. The Indians cried out. And suddenly they were all yelling and shrieking, and the air was filled with clutching fingers and flashing knives. The brown bodies shoved and crushed and surged against the white men.

Delk struck out blindly. "Help, Hurdly, help!" he bellowed and a huge hand seized him by the throat.

# Chapter 10

# The warning sign in the sky

he jockey shrieked like a pig caught under a fence. He climbed right up Delk till the boy was nearly blinded by red hair and hands and fists and arms and his ears were deafened by Jamie's steady yells as the Indians jerked and tugged at the Englishman's shining head.

Delk was struggling to reach the fingers that had him by the throat before his neck was pulled right out from between his head and his body. He knocked away that hand, but a dozen others were clinging to him. It was as frustrating and useless as fighting feathers, and he feared for his Adam's apple.

He was pulled roughly aside, at least some of him was. How much stayed behind he wasn't sure, but suddenly he was free of the poking fingers and the heavy bodies and left staggering on the fringe. It took him a moment to recover. He saw Jamie disappear under a mass of Saponi and heard his sad, despairing wail. The Indians were killing him, Delk was certain. He leaped back into the fray. He had to help!

He clutched at the nearest bare arm, but it popped right out of his grasp. He shoved at what looked almost like a wall of solid flesh and went sliding off. The Indians were too well greased with bear's oil. He could neither hold them nor move them.

"Help, help," he bawled again. The greasy bodies swirled away from him for a moment, and he had a glimpse of Jamie's red hair. He dived after him.

The Englishman needed no help, however. Biting, kicking, and squirming, he slid through a warren of legs and was suddenly free of the Indians. He dodged a dozen outstretched hands and flew across the square, leaped onto a block of wood and from there to one of the flat roofs. He lost no time in scurrying over and down on the outside and away from the town. With his shirt tails flying behind him and his bright queue standing out from his head, he looked like one of the huge woodpeckers Delk sometimes saw in the forests.

Delk would have fled himself, only he was surrounded by Indians who were behaving in such a strange way that he had to stop and look. They were staggering around holding their sides and leaning against each other—and roaring with laughter. There was Hurdly Lane along with them, wiping his eyes and shaking his head and looking pleased as a cat in cream. For a minute Delk was furious. Then slowly he began to grin. It had been funny, after all, especially the sight of Jamie flying over the roofs.

He was ashamed of himself for getting scared. After all he'd said to Pigg about the peaceful Saponi. He'd been taken in for fair.

"Whoooo-ppeee!" shouted Lane. "Did you ever see anything like that? The little feller was five feet off the ground all across here! And you ought to have seen yourself, Rogers, your eyes was most nigh out of your head. Oh, that was a good one on you both. I never planned on the hair, you know. I never reckoned it would get them so riled up. Oh, ho, ho! What a joke!"

Delk laughed. "It was a pretty good one," he admitted. "And Jamie Pigg makes fair game. I never saw a human being come so close to growing wings and flying." He paused and looked at Lane. "But he ain't got that red thatch of hair for nothing, Hurdly. I reckon there's a bad temper somewhere under it. Once you get him ired enough, I'll lay he can play a few tricks of his own."

Hurdly pitched a pair of moccasins to him. "I'll chance it," he grinned and went whistling off through the town. Delk watched him go. Maybe Hurdly Lane wouldn't think it so funny if the tables were turned and he was the one the trick was played on. That might be something to ponder. In the meanwhile Delk figured he might as well make the best of things and enjoy the way Hurdly livened up the dull days at the fort. He turned and left through a passageway, laughing.

When Delk got back to the barracks, he found the little English-man with his carbine in his hands, scowling ferociously. He paused in the doorway, not sure whether it was safe to enter. Jamie looked up.

"You're not aiming to shoot anybody, are you?" Delk asked. Jamie had taken little interest in his gun before. He'd never even shot it once. "It was a joke, Jamie. But Lane never counted on your hair setting 'em so wild. His diddle worked a heap better than he planned. I was scared witless myself."

"You was?" the jockey asked doubtfully. "Blimey, I thought I was a goner." He sighed. "I reckon I made a running fool of meself once more. And 'twas simple of me, for I guessed 'e 'ad some sort of swindle in mind."

"Well, Lane never cheated you out of the shoes anyway," Delk said and placed them on the Englishman's bed.

Jamie paid no attention. He stood staring down at the carbine in his hands. At last he spoke. "I 'ates it," he said slowly. "I 'ates being so skittish, like a 'orse that's got a burr under its tail. And I 'ates this place, these 'ere trees and snakes and all. But 'ere I am. I got to stay for fifty-seven days more. I've made up me mind. I'll be the best ranger there is, afore I'm done. I'll learn to shoot and to spy out red Injuns and kill panthers with me bare 'ands."

Delk laughed. "Great day in the morning!" he cried. "That's fine news, and I reckon I can help a mite and we might as well get started right now."

Pigg's carbine was rusty, and Delk spent some time cleaning the inside of the barrel and picking loose the powder caked in the touchhole and making sure the lock worked properly. Then he showed the jockey how to make cartridges with paper and string, lead balls and powder. The next morning he and Jamie took a walk into the woods, downstream from the horse pen. There was a clearing there which some of the rangers occasionally used for shooting, wagering they could hit a fly's eye at twenty paces and making all kinds of wild wagers on their shots.

Delk made a target of a shingle with a mud spot in the center and wedged this into the bark of a tree. He paced off a distance and stationed Jamie in front of it.

"Put the hammer back to half cock and take a paper cartridge from your cartouche box," Delk instructed. "Now bite off the end where the powder is."

Jamie did as he was told, and as he bit into the paper he squealed, "Rotten tooth!" He bit again and poured a little powder into the priming pan and closed it.

"Put the rest of the powder in the barrel and ram the ball and paper down on top of it," Delk went on. "Don't hurry. Do it slow and get the ball right down on the powder."

"I'll never do all this if the red Indians was shooting at me," Jamie said gloomily. "Never."

Delk wasn't sure he would either, since he'd never been in battle. It'd be his luck to drop the ramrod or forget to prime the gun. "Pull the hammer all the way back and it's ready to shoot." He helped Jamie settle it comfortably against his shoulder. "Aim down the barrel at the black spot and give fire."

Jamie shot and the shingle fell. "A hit first off," shouted Delk.

"I've watched the lords and fine gentlemen 'andle fowling pieces at their shoots," shrugged Jamie. "It don't seem that almighty different. I just never much took to it, you see. Me ears don't like the din, for one thing."

"You get used to it," Delk promised.

They practiced when they could for the next few days, then Delk left on a range. When he got back two days later, he looked up Jamie first thing. "We'll shoot a bit more tomorrow," he said. "Maybe go hunting."

Tupper was standing by. "Captain won't like it," he put in. "Tomorrow's Mr. Griffin's Sunday and you know as well as I do the Captain don't hold with firearms then."

Jamie said soberly, " 'E's right too. Remember the Lord's day and keep it 'oly."

One Sunday a month the Reverend Griffin stayed at the fort to hold a service and preach a sermon. The other three Sundays in the month he traveled to neighboring plantations or to the Saponi town. Some of the rangers helped to arrange the benches and tables in the schoolroom for use as a place of worship. Hurdly and Delk were commissioned to carry Will Crumbly, the ranger whose leg had been broken in his fall from a rearing horse, to hear the minister.

"I can't see no reason for it," complained Hurdly. "It ain't like you couldn't hear the Reverend Griffin plain as day right in the barracks. He's got a voice like a dying buffalo."

"Ow, ow, careful now," warned Crumbly. "Well, Lane, a old sinner like you wouldn't be reckoned to know how it is. It does a sick man good to go to church. You watch out now, Rogers, afore I pull your ears down around your neck. It don't feel so sweet to be joggled around like that. And anyway, I ain't been out of the barracks for two weeks and it's a fair treat to see the sky again."

But on the journey back to the barracks the sky was suddenly darkened and there was a whistling, windy sound. A storm? Delk glanced up. No, it was a vast flock of pigeons, a mass of them, solid from rim to rim. Delk had never seen such a number.

"Now, whoa, there!" bawled Will. "You done almost dropped me! Ain't you never seen pigeons before?"

"I ain't," whispered Jamie, who was walking with them. "Not like that I ain't. It fair makes my flesh creep. So many is against nature, that's what it is."

"You're right there," Crumbly put in. "It's a bad sign. My pappy used to say the devil was chasing 'em. Anyway, it always means bad luck and bad days. The week before my pappy passed away of a fever, a flock like this one went over."

"Oh, forevermore," cried Lane impatiently. "It don't mean a thing but good hunting and good eating. Let 'em go to roost, I'll fetch ten sackfuls back to the cooks and we'll eat us a pigeon pie like you ain't never et before."

Delk moved along toward the barracks, shifting his hands under Crumbly's weight. "How come we don't just shoot 'em now?" he asked.

"'Twouldn't do no good," Hurdly asserted. "Them birds is packed so tight together, no matter how many you hit, they wouldn't fall. They're just squeezed up solid, dead ones just get carried along with the rest, still beating their wings in time with all the others."

Jamie looked awed. Delk laughed. "Ain't he the finest liar you ever listened to?" he asked the jockey. But as Delk and Hurdly lifted Will to his bed the injured ranger proclaimed loudly, "Lane's a liar, but I ain't. Them pigeons mean bad times, you wait and bear me out."

The next day Crumbly's leg began to swell and mortify. He

groaned and moaned, and Mr. Griffin came to treat him every few hours. The weather grew hot and sullen, and two of the rangers came down with ague, shaking and shivering one day, burning with fever the next. Delk hated to go in the barracks there was so much misery there.

He volunteered for every patrol and acquitted himself well enough in the woods. At least he did nothing wrong, but since he encountered few living things except very fat ground hogs and crows and jays, he hardly had much of an opportunity to make a mistake. Each time he returned, Jamie greeted him with the number of days left for him to stay in this savage land as a ranger.

It saddened Delk. He was getting quite attached to the little Englishman and hated to be reminded that soon the two of them would be going different ways, parted forever.

Too, Jamie's counting off the days kept reminding Delk that he had to make up his mind soon about what to do when his term of enlistment was finished. The only decision he'd made was that he wasn't going home. Other than that he hadn't the least notion what work he might do or whether he should try some trade. He felt sure he could do almost anything. He was getting more confident. He hadn't done a single careless thing for two weeks and it pleased him immensely.

Will Crumbly had to be moved to Williamsburg to be doctored, and another man came down with chills and fever. It was a bad time to have so many rangers unable to ride, for often in the fall of the year, especially if the weather held warm, the Indians went raiding and warring. Commander Flood was in a flurry. He no longer held musters and often went on patrol himself. One morning he appeared beside Delk and demanded, "Where's Pigg?"

"I believe he's down at the horse pen," Delk replied.

"Well, fetch him," cried Flood. "You and he will have to ride out today, just the two of you. I'll give you an assignment where trouble's not likely, but somebody's got to watch. And you two are all I've got right now."

But down at the horse pen Jamie refused to go. One of the horses had the blackwater. " 'E'll die, less somebody keeps him walking," said Jamie. "His back legs is well nigh paralyzed now."

"I reckon he's right," said the commander dolefully, when Delk reported the news. "We need horses as bad as men. Well, Rogers, you'll have to go alone. I'll give you three of the best Saponi scouts."

Delk was far from pleased at the order. He was still haunted by the thought that some careless act of his might endanger the lives of plantation folks and settlers. When he had other rangers with him, the danger was not great. But all alone? It gave him a deep uneasy feeling in the pit of his stomach.

Still, there was no shirking. It had to be done, and he would make the very best job he could of it. His two days in the woods with the Saponi were a strain on him. He jumped at every rustle and creak and lay awake most of the night worrying.

"I'm just like Jamie, that first night after we left Williamsburg," he thought, staring up at the sky, bright with fall stars. "But I keep remembering how an Injun war party might come slipping up."

On the morning of the third day he returned to the fort. He was feeling tired but quite proud of himself. He had done everything that his duty required and hadn't failed in any detail. There'd been no sign of enemy Indians and there was nothing to report to Captain Flood.

A mile or so from the fort he met Tupper and his Indian scouts. They had been tracking some Senecas who had captured a plantation servant.

"We lost 'em," said Tupper wearily as they splashed across the Meherrin River. "They got in among them hills and valleys to the west and I doubt the devil himself could find 'em there."

At the horse pen Delk looked about for Jamie, but the little redhead wasn't there. He wasn't at the brush arbor he'd built at the edge of the woods to shelter the sick horse.

Delk was too tired to look further. He rubbed Nuck down rather hastily with a handful of straw and fed him. He slung the saddle to his shoulder and headed up the hill toward the fort.

Tupper caught up with him. "You're in a hurry," he said. "You ain't even took the cockleburs out of poor old Nuck's tail."

"I'll do it later," said Delk. "I've got to get me some rest now. I'm plumb dizzy-headed."

At the gate they met Stryker coming out, tightly wrapped in a blanket.

"What ails you?" asked Tupper, staring at the blanket.

Stryker gave a violent shudder. "I reckon I got me the fever," he said hollowly. "I'm going to the sweat house."

Delk watched him go off. "Sweating—does that work for white men too?" he asked. Tupper shrugged. "No telling what works for Stryker," he answered. "He's a strange one, anyway you look at him."

Captain Hix was standing on the gun platform next to the ranger headquarters along with two Indians. Delk squinted at the red men. They were not Saponi he felt sure.

"Occaneechies," Tupper told him. "That's Chief Hanging White Man. They sure do love them cannon."

"They ought to have to clean the things once in a while," said Delk shortly and passed on across the yard to enter his barracks. He flung his saddle in the corner and fell on his bed. But then he roused himself and looked around for Jamie. There was no sign of the jockey. His carbine and cartridge box were missing. Had Jamie gone hunting by himself? Delk wondered. Surely not. He must be out practicing, that was all. And Delk fell promptly asleep.

He woke an hour or so later, feeling better. There was still no sign of Jamie Pigg. Delk asked one of the other rangers if he'd seen Jamie that day. "Not since breakfast," the man answered.

Delk shrugged. He strolled down to the horse pen to tend to Nuck, to comb out the cockleburs and treat the scratch on the horse's flank. On the way he turned aside to the brush arbor for the ailing horse. Had Jamie taken the horse into the woods? Delk walked in among the trees.

The horse was lying on the ground, half-hidden by undergrowth. It was dead, its belly ripped open and its guts spilled out. Wolves! Wolves had done this. They were quick to know when a helpless horse was around. Delk bent to look and there were their big dog-like tracks.

He followed them a way and stopped in horror. Beside the wolves' prints were Jamie Pigg's neat little footmarks. A tiny man like Jamie against a pack of full grown wolves? He didn't stand a chance!

# Chapter 11

# *Wolves and bears*

*D*elk ran as hard as he could and every now and then he groaned to himself. Poor little Jamie! An awful way to die, with his throat torn out by those slavering jaws. Delk remembered coming on a wolf's skull in the woods not too long ago and he shuddered recalling those long white teeth. Oh, Lordee!

The trail was easy to follow, for there had been a great many wolves. Through the trees and around a low swampy place he sped, and on into a pine grove. He lost the tracks on the thick bed of needles and hunted frantically around the edge of the grove till he picked it up again.

Oh, he hoped he was in time. He'd heard so many tales of men and horses attacked by wolves. And children! Children were always being carried off by wolves—and Jamie was no bigger than a child.

He dashed in among some bushes and a deer leaped away with a startled flash of white tail. Mast was plentiful this year; acorns and hickory nuts lay thick under the trees, and it was hard running across them. His feet twisted this way and that and once went flying right out from under him. He whammed the ground hard and after that he slowed down.

What would give Pigg the idea he could deal with a pack of wolves anyway? They were the meanest varmints around. "But it's likely my fault," thought Delk guiltily. "I was always dinging at him about standing up to things and not being scared. But you'd think he'd know better than to go against a pack of grown wolves, a little tiny fellow like that."

He speeded up once again. He *had* to be in time to try to save the jockey. Oh, why hadn't he gone to look for him as soon as he'd returned to the fort this morning? Why did he have to sleep the morning away while the wolves crushed poor Jamie's bones?

On and on he pounded. The wolves had veered toward the river, and Delk could see plainly where they had splashed along its edge, sliding and slipping across a mud flat and playing about in the water. At a point where the Meherrin forked into many little rippling channels through a mass of tumbled rocks, the band had forded. Delk crossed to the other side but lost the trail. The land rose sharply, the ground was stony and dry, and tracking was impossible.

All at once it came over him that there had been no sign of Jamie's tracks along the riverbank. He tried to remember how far back he'd last seen the jockey's prints, but he couldn't. Perhaps he'd passed the Englishman, lying under a bush, ripped, torn, and bleeding, and he'd never noticed, he'd been rushing along so fast. If Jamie were dead then he, Delk, was to blame, he thought miserably and moaned aloud. He hadn't realized how fond he'd gotten of the little man or how much he would miss him.

Recrossing the river, he hurried back over the route he'd traveled. But he couldn't go on, he was much too tired. No proper sleep on the range and now all this hard running. He had to rest. He lay still and by and by got his breath back and his heart slowed to its normal pace. In the wood's silence a tomtit called and then he heard a sound like voices. He sat up listening.

It *was* voices. He jumped to his feet. Men were talking not far away, several of them, and there was something familiar about the sound of one. It wasn't Jamie, but it was somebody from the fort. He'd get whoever it was to help hunt for the jockey. He almost called out then, but something about that one voice stopped him. Instead he crawled forward and crouched behind a fallen tree, peering out cautiously.

In a little clearing five men squatted in a circle, two white men and three Indians. Delk knew the red men weren't Saponi, and he had a suspicion they might be Tuscaroras. One of the white men was a stranger, but the other, the one with his back to Delk, seemed familiar. Suddenly this man spoke.

"Stryker!" breathed Delk to himself. "It *is* Stryker!" He'd been right about that voice. "But what's he doing out here? He's supposed to be at Saponi Town sweating his sickness away."

Stryker didn't seem sick now. He spoke out in a harsh voice. "They can trust me, they know they can, I done showed it." The other white man stared at him a moment and then said something in another tongue. The braves nodded.

"You can tell them it will be in three weeks. Here, I'll fix a stick for them," Stryker went on, grabbing up a fallen branch and sliding the bark from it. "You make 'em see I can be trusted," he added fiercely. "This means a heap to me and to a certain high and mighty man in the Colony. I've got this land surveyed already. If the Saponi leave, it'll be ours, every bit. Tell them I can let their tribe have more goods than they ever knew was around and still end up a rich man."

The other man grinned at him. "You got things fixed up proper, ain't you?" he said admiringly and turned back to the Indians. Stryker worked away at his stick, carving notches one after another. Just like that war stick the Seneca warrior had carried this summer, Delk told himself.

What could it all mean? How could Stryker be a rich man? How had he shown whom that he could be trusted? And who was this important man Stryker was working with in this? Delk crawled quietly away. Whatever Stryker was up to the boy knew well it was not honest. He didn't want to be caught spying. He had a feeling that Stryker wouldn't think twice about slitting his throat if he threatened to interfere with these plans. Stryker was full of wickedness, Delk had known it all along even if Captain Flood hadn't.

He sneaked off quickly and didn't stop sliding on his stomach till there was a little hill between him and Stryker and those Indians. He didn't know what to make of what he'd heard, but he had not time now to stop and ponder on it. He had to get along and find Jamie.

He headed toward the river, but walk as hard as he would, he couldn't find the Meherrin. He turned counter and hurried off in that direction, but had to fetch up fast and admit he was in a part of the wood that was completely strange to him and with no water in sight.

From ahead of him came a sudden moan and a deep snoring growl, followed by Jamie's voice, sad and thin, "Ow, ow, ow! Leave me be. Them be my toes, watch, ow! Now leave off, you hear me?"

Delk didn't have far to look. In the first place, Jamie had left a clear trail, first one moccasin, then another, then his big hat. In the second place, the jockey kept up a steady lamentation. "Oh, oh, where was my 'ead when I thought to leave London?" he wailed. " 'Twasn't on my shoulder, and that's a fact. Oh, oh, ow, I wish I'd died in me cradle."

The bear came into view first, the biggest bear he'd ever seen in his life. She sat on top of Jamie's carbine at the foot of a hackberry tree, her snout pointed upwards and her little eyes twinkling with rage. From her throat came a long, loud snarl.

Jamie, very much alive and unharmed by any wolf teeth or claws, was up in the tree, but he was not alone. Right below him a bear cub clung to the trunk and every now and then pawed at Jamie's bare feet or snuffled at them with a black nose and pink tongue. Then the Englishman shinnied up higher. The cub followed and Jamie edged away from it. The bear persisted in joining him and the jockey gave it a fierce slap. And slap went the cub's paw in return. Slap, slap, what a game! Delk could tell the cub enjoyed this new playmate. Whopping each other and scrambling from limb to limb, the two climbed higher and higher.

It was the funniest thing Delk had ever seen in his life, funny enough to make a dead man laugh for sure. And all the while the two small figures frisked about above, the vast mother bear sat beneath uttering ugly threats and warnings.

Delk almost whooped out with laughter, but not quite. For the first time he realized that he had come down to the horse pen empty-handed and he was still empty-handed! A mother bear was nothing to joke about, and if matters worsened he could do nothing whatsoever to help Jamie Pigg. A stick, a rock—all he had—would be nothing against this mountain of fat.

The two were near the top of the hackberry now. The trunk swayed and bent and the little bear had to scramble to keep its hold. But Jamie wasn't doing too well at holding on either. It looked almost like a contest to see which would shake the other out. The big bear didn't like it, seemingly, for she reared up on her hind legs and gave the tree a bang or two.

Jamie shrieked and mounted a little higher. The thin trunk bent slowly to one side. Seeing this, Jamie decided to back down, but the cub was right below him, once more nuzzling at his toes. In a panic Jamie drew his feet away from the cub's snout. There was a quick terrifying crack, and the top of the tree, Jamie, and the cub were all hurtling down through the air.

The whole tangled mess landed on the big bear. Delk yelled in terror, but he didn't dare go any closer. Squealing and protesting, the mother staggered to one side, wiping away tree and jockey and furry offspring. The cub kicked its legs about for a moment, then jumped up and went dashing off. The mama bear lumbered after.

At once Delk leaped toward the motionless body of Jamie Pigg. The little man was white as a corpse, his eyes were half-open and blank, and his chest wasn't moving. "Oh, Jamie, Jamie!" cried Delk.

The jockey drew a great strangling breath. "Me wind," he gasped. "Knocked out of me."

Delk grinned in relief and helped Pigg sit up. In a few minutes Jamie seemed to recover. "You all right?" Delk asked.

A flush spread over Jamie's face. "All right?" he cried. "I been chased by wild animals and spent 'alf a lifetime up a tree with one of 'em and done fell out on me 'ead on top of a terrible great bear, and you want to know am I all right? No, I ain't. I'm scared to death and that cub done bit off me toes and the big one done trompled my innards and I ain't all right."

Delk grinned more than ever. "Oh, you're a champion, Jamie Pigg," he exclaimed. "I would never have thought to get rid of a bear by falling on it. 'Twas a master stroke and I'm terrible proud of you."

The little jockey said nothing. He bent to examine his toes, which were still there in spite of what he'd said. "Well, I never went to do it," he confessed at last. "You 'adn't ought to joke about such things. I just may never be able to get up on me legs again, for I'm weak as a kitten."

He began to grin and in a minute or two he and Delk were both rocking with laughter. After a while Delk collected Jamie's moccasins and hat and picked up the carbine. He inspected it and handed it to the jockey. "I reckon that old bear would have shot you out of the tree if she had any cartridges," he snickered. "Where's your cartouche box?"

They found it among the bushes, and then they started for the fort. Delk was sure he wasn't lost but he might just have to do some wandering around to get back. That wouldn't be too good if Stryker was still about in the woods. Stryker might be worse than the she bear.

"Did you try to shoot that bear?" Delk asked on the way.

"La, there was no time to cock the gun and aim and do all those things," Jamie exclaimed. "That old she took against me soon as ever she laid eyes on me and she come straight for me. I just took out running, flinging things left and right and I ran right up the first tree I come to—," he paused, shaking his head in amazement. "Ran right up the trunk, mind you, too scared to stop and climb up and that cub ran up the trunk along beside me."

Delk smiled. That would have been something to see. "It wouldn't have done you any good to shoot at that bear anyway," he said. "Bears that big, with all that winter fat and hair, you got to get up close and shoot 'em in the ear."

"I wasn't likely to get so close," snorted Jamie. "Bears ain't no decent company for a Henglishman. Mamas nor their young 'uns neither. I 'ates to think what that cub would 'ave done to me if you 'adn't 'appened along."

"I didn't do a thing," Delk pointed out. "You fell on the old critter all by yourself. Ah, it was a clever thing to do. You're a real woodsman, Jamie. You see, I told you you'd learn."

"And 'ere we be out in the woods with wolves and bears, just strolling along calm as you please," went on Jamie. But Delk noticed that the jockey really didn't seem to be much alarmed at the idea. He didn't look around at every sound of the wind or every crackling twig. Maybe he really *was* learning. Certainly he was bristling with bravery when they passed the dead horse.

"Them wolves!" Jamie cried indignantly. "Them wicked wolves! I went to tend to my poor old 'orse and they'd been at the ailing beast and killed it dead. I lost me temper, I did, and I fetched my piece and went after them. But I ain't too good at trailing such things and lost their tracks soon enough."

He looked down at the horse and shook his head sadly. "Poor old quidder," he breathed. "Not much good for riding. Jog your gizzard loose, but she was a good friend the days I worked at the pen."

Wolves and bears and Stryker—the woods had been full of varmints this day, mused Delk. They were lucky to be back at the fort alive and safe. "Come along," he said, trotting up the hill. "I'm about to die of hunger."

# Chapter 12

# *Arrival of the Occaneechi*

ell, what's it mean?" asked Delk. He dropped a log on the fire and watched the sparks shoot up the barracks chimney.

"It means," replied Tupper, "that come December first, Captain Hix and his trader bunch'll be leaving Fort Christanna just like us rangers."

Delk turned away from the hearth. Tupper was just back from Williamsburg and this was the news he brought. It had fairly upset the whole fort and the Indians of Saponi Town too.

"The Burgesses has raised a clamor against the Indian company— they aim to repeal the act that set it up. That's the rumor anyway," Tupper added, beginning to refill his pipe. "I reckon nobody knows for sure."

"There goes my grand scheme," said Hurdly gloomily, raking his chestnuts out of the ashes. "I aimed to sign on with Hix for guard duty. Bound to be easy for a man that's been a ranger nigh on to two years."

Delk cracked a beechnut with his teeth. Jamie looked up from cleaning his carbine and stared at the flames. "At 'ome men go to sea when they can't get no other work," he asserted. "I could have shipped back to England that way, but I dast not. It's a terrible 'ard life and I was seasick all the way over."

Hurdly looked shaken. "Go to sea! Me?" he cried. "I'd as soon hire out as a pack horse."

Delk thought he would too. He'd never been on a ship, but he'd seen one. Think of being confined to that little space for weeks and weeks with nothing but water to stare at. Think of having people boss you about every minute of the day. He couldn't stand it. Those officers would be worse than four sisters. At least his sisters never beat him with belaying pins.

"How come you want guard duty for the Indian company?" he asked Hurdly. "How come you don't want to go west and trade?"

"On account of I don't want to," replied Hurdly shortly and Delk looked at him suddenly. Hurdly had always been the only one of the rangers on good terms with Stryker. Were they in this scheme, whatever it might be, together? Did Hurdly mean to stay on here at Christanna to help Stryker with his plans? Delk wished there was somebody he could talk to about all this. Maybe what Stryker had in mind was honest, but it didn't seem likely, knowing Stryker.

Delk had hoped to talk Hurdly into going amongst the Indians with him, but not the way things stood now, he wouldn't. He'd have to look around for somebody else. There was bound to be one here willing to go with him.

"Me, I aim to go trading," Delk said finally. "I'll spend my wages for trinkets and goods and go west, over past the mountains where the buffaloes are thick as fleas. That trader that got back yesterday —what's his name, Overbury—he says there's a new passage through the mountains leading right to them buffaloes. He showed me a buffalo skin all painted over with Injun pictures and signs. Buffalo . . . "

In his mind he could see a great savannah covered with them. And there he was walking among them leading his pack horses to the Indian town at the far side of the savannah. He could see the chief coming out to meet him and welcoming him with presents.

One of the other men, a tall, skinny fellow named Proctor, dug his hand into his shirt and pulled out a rock. He laid it on his palm and held it out to the others. "Looky there, what Overbury give me!" he cried. "Gold! And he can tell where he got it, for a price."

Hurdly spit into the fire. "Gold!" he cried sarcastically. "You think he'd give it to you if 'twas real gold? I seen that stuff before. And I've heard that tale about gold mines—and about lead mines and silver mines and every other kind of mine. All them traders know for sure where mines be, they just can't recollect long enough to guide folks to 'em.' "

"What d'ye mean, it ain't gold?" Proctor answered furiously. "Look how it sparkles!"

Delk didn't pay any attention. He was still a thousand miles away, dreaming of wide meadows and buffalo hides, clear rivers and high blue mountains. Oh, he'd made up his mind. As soon as the ranger company was dissolved and he drew his pay, he meant to go west and see it all for himself.

Hurdly's hard hand on his shoulder woke him from his reverie. "Where you at, Rogers?" he asked, shaking him roughly. "I done told you twice, Captain Flood says you and me got to cut firewood tomorrow."

"What for?" asked Jamie. "There's wood in plenty stacked outside 'ere."

"For them Occaneechies coming to treaty talk," Hurdly explained.

"Oh, aye," Jamie nodded. "I recollect."

"You better recollect," Tupper said sourly to him. "We're all going to be doing extra guard duty and running and fetching while they're here. And Flood'll want everything done just so, for it'll be his last chance to be the commander at such doings here; he'll want it all to go like clockwork."

Delk didn't know how Jamie had ever forgotten, for both Captain Hix and Commander Flood were making a fuss about the Indians coming to talk. The Occaneechi's headmen had picked the spot for their camp, close to a spring on a little savannah just back of the fort. Tupper had brought back a message from the Virginia Council to go ahead with the meeting, whether the trading company was dissolved or not, it would help the colony to have the friendly Indians on its southern frontier as a protection. So Captain Hix was most anxious that the visitors should feel welcome and have a good supply of water and wood and food while they were here.

Delk had tried some time past to explain to Jamie that the Occaneechi were kin to the Saponi and that this Occaneechi town way off down in Carolina had decided to move close to the fort,

though they did not want to live in Saponi Town. Indians were always shifting their towns, as far as Delk could see, no place ever
seemed to please them. But to get the Occaneechi to settle near Fort
Christanna would take a lot of petitions and talk and conferences
before everything was arranged to satisfaction for all parties.

"Will the governor be 'ere?" asked Jamie. Delk shook his head
and told him, "They're just getting up a petition to send to the governor. Captain Hix and the interpreter'll have to write it all out neat
and proper first."

"A pity not to see 'im again," Jamie went on. "He looked to be a
fine civilized gentleman riding around Williamsburg."

"He's that," nodded Hurdly, "and he knows how to get along
with the red savages too. But if he was here, we'd have twice the
work."

"When'll this meeting be?" asked the jockey.

"A week, maybe a day or so beyond, I reckon," Hurdly yawned.
"Tupper, you and Proctor get back to your own barracks and let
us get some rest."

Delk was quick to wrap up in his blankets. But he wasn't quick
to get to sleep. For the longest he lay awake, listening to the cold
November wind whistle down the chimney, planning and planning
how he would go away to the marvelous waiting lands to the west.

"Fall out! Fall out! They're coming!" bellowed Captain Flood.

Jamie and Delk were the first out in the yard. Jamie had been
dressed and ready with his gear all about him, for some time. The
impending arrival of the Indians and the ceremony to accompany
it had filled him with interest.

The other rangers were not so eager. "On the quick!" thundered
Flood and the rest began to emerge from the barracks. Slowly and
without enthusiasm they lined up at the gate, along with some of
the trading company men. They had done it all before, often, and
they were not looking forward to seeing it all another time.

"Two lines, let's go!" ordered the commander.

He and Captain Hix stood to one side, their boots and weapons
polished to a shine, their coats brushed and the ruffles starched. To
their left and a step behind stood Captain Captain, decked out in his

finest clothes and wearing bright red and yellow ribbons braided in his hair.

Stryker was on the cannon platform, standing at attention with the linstock, holding the slow match at his side. The fuse smoldered and sent long streamers of smoke around Stryker's face. Delk thought he looked like the devil himself.

From far off came the sound of drums and once in a while a high-pitched yelp. "Is that a war 'oop?" asked Jamie a little anxiously.

Delk shook his head. "That's their kind of singing, I reckon," he told him.

The sound of drums grew louder, and the Indians came in sight through the open gate. They marched in single file and the chief, Hanging White Man, led the procession. He wore a yellow jerkin and a matchcoat of beaver skins around his shoulders. His hair was shiny with bear oil, hawk bells jingled from his ears, and a cutlass was thrust through his broad red sash.

"Corblimy, 'e's grand," whispered Jamie. " 'E looks like a prince, 'e do."

The two drummers came next, tapping on their small skin drums, and then a warrior with a great painted-gourd rattle which he shook in rhythm with his steps. Behind these came the rest of the braves, dressed in softly cured skins and ornaments and shirts of colored silks and duffield. They stalked in with proud faces and dignified carriage. Oh, they did look fine stepping along, and Jamie was impressed, Delk could tell. He stared at them solemnly.

"Poise firelock!" commanded Flood, and the men in the two lines cocked their pieces and held the guns upright before them. At the order "Present!" each man raised his gun to his shoulder and pointed it toward the sky.

The Occaneechi walked slowly and gravely between the two lines of rangers. "Fire!" bawled Captain Flood.

There was a mingled sound of many guns and then a single shot sounding after all the rest. Jamie had fired the belated shot. He'd grown so interested in the Indians he had hardly realized where he was. He grew red and looked flustered when the captain gave him a disgusted look.

The Indians passed to the end of the lines, turned about and stood waiting.

The captain nodded to Stryker, who held the linstock high and, wheeling stiffly, stepped up close to the cannon. He lowered the slow match and blew on it. When the fuse turned cherry red, he held it down to the touchhole. There was a sputter and a trail of smoke, and then a "Whoom!" that shook the earth. For a minute a cloud of evil-smelling blue haze enveloped Stryker and the cannon before drifting away.

For the first time the Indians' faces ceased to be masks of impassive dignity. They grinned excitedly, one or two cried out in delight, and they raised their own guns and fired them in a return salute.

It was the last time they would fire the guns for several days. Now they must give them to the rangers for safekeeping. Delk was one of the ones assigned to collect the guns. He was glad, it kept him from having to listen to Captain Flood, who was now making a flowery speech that went on and on. Finally the commander shut up, and Hanging White Man answered with another long speech. Then Captain Hix spoke and gave each of the red men a white clay pipe and a twist of tobacco and bade them rest from their journey and eat heartily of the meat cooking at their campsite.

The Occaneechi chief responded with great politeness and after finishing presented a matchcoat of otter skins to Captain Flood and one to Captain Hix. Now Captain Captain stepped forward and a ranger groaned, "Is he going to get to speechify too?" However the Saponi chief only spoke briefly and then led the visitors off to their camp.

"Blimy!" exclaimed Jamie. "That was grand, that was."

Delk was surprised. "What do you mean, grand?" he questioned. "It was just some Injuns and the same old thing from the captains."

Jamie scratched his head. "I dunno," he confessed. "But it was like—well, it wasn't like nothing. It was—grand, that's all. It was like last month when the trees turned all them fine grand colors." That was the best he could do at telling Delk how it was.

"Well, I reckon you won't think it's so grand when the work starts piling up," said Delk grimly. "We'll have plenty to do, guarding the camp and all. When the Injuns come visiting, they're always glad to let white men fetch and carry for 'em. We'll be doing everything but lighting their pipes for 'em. And Jamie, you best get busy cleaning that cannon bore. Stryker will stick you inside it and shoot you over the mountains if you don't hurry with it."

That night the Indians used most of the wood Hurdly and Delk had cut to build a huge fire. The Occaneechi and the Saponi danced around it, whooping and yelling. Then one of the rangers played a fiddle and the Indians rolled on the ground with laughter at the sounds. There was much talk and laughter. Delk went to bed early for he was tired, but he could hear the sounds still going on when he woke in the darkness. Jamie was climbing into bed, having stayed late to see and hear what he could.

The next day he told Delk, "The chief, 'e got that name from a dream 'e 'ad, 'e did. Dreamed 'e saw three white men 'anging in a row. Fancy being named for a dream! I was named for me uncle."

"You and me, we got guard duty tonight," Delk answered glumly. "Midnight on. I'd like to hang Stryker for putting us on that."

Jamie shrugged as though a guard assignment meant nothing to him. "Named for a dream," he repeated in amazement.

The Indian camp was quiet when Jamie and Delk relieved the other two rangers who had been on guard. A chilly wind was blowing, but it was bright moonlight. The fire still burned, as Delk knew it would continuously till the visitors left. A couple of braves sat smoking nearby, but most of the Occaneechi lay sleeping under the two canvas marquees which had been provided for them.

A dog from the Saponi village came aimlessly into the circle of firelight, and Delk flung a rock at it to make it scamper off. The braves paused in their puffing and looked toward him. Then it was quiet again. Delk walked softly along the distance assigned to him for patrol. How still it was here, here under the trees, away from the campfire, not even a cricket creaked. It was dark as the inside of a hat, too. He went forward slowly to avoid falling over anything or stepping into the creek that trickled away from the spring.

Six months ago he would never have dreamed that now he would be doing such a thing. Six months ago he had been faced with a life of crops, of plowing and harvesting, and caring for his family's land and animals.

But not any more. He'd been discontented even then, and now he knew why. The world was too wide and exciting and full of things to spend it tied to one little acreage. He meant to travel far and wide over the blue edge of the world before he grew much older. To hunt deer and buffalo and heaven only knew what other strange things in the territory to the west, to see the great Mississippi River maybe, and the curious country beyond it. To see these things for himself, not just listen to tales other folks brought back.

He was wondering whether he could buy another horse and how much trade goods two could tote, when he was aware that someone was moving ahead of him. Even though part of his mind had been wandering, the rest had still been alert and his fingers tightened on his gun. "Who's there?" he growled.

The shadow, a darkness in the darkness, halted. After a minute Stryker's voice came softly, "That you, Rogers?"

"It's me," answered Delk.

Stryker whispered again, "Come over here, Rogers. Something's going on. I need some help."

Obediently Delk went forward. He strained his eyes. The shadow he'd thought was Stryker seemed to have disappeared. He took another cautious step. "Stryker, where are you?" he asked. Something moved beside him and a thousand stars exploded before his eyes.

# Chapter 13

# *Arrows and bullets*

D elk stared up at the moon, riding peacefully among the bare branches of the trees. Dream-like he seemed to float with it until he shifted and a flash of pain shot through his head. Why was he lying here in the night on the cold mossy earth? How did he come to be here? And where in creation was he anyway? Ooo, how his head ached!

There was a great amount of noise coming from somewhere, shrieks and popping sounds like gunshots. He touched a knot over his ear, a big knot. Stryker! He remembered now, Stryker had tricked him. Stryker had raised this lump on the side of his head. He sat up quickly and then groaned and grabbed his head.

Why had Stryker hit him anyway? It didn't make sense. There was something hard under his leg and he felt around and found it to be his carbine. Guard duty! How long ago was that, he wondered.

The early morning was filled with people, all running and shouting. What was happening? Tupper and Hurdly hurried by, very close, shouting, "Senecas! Over here! In the woods!" Then those really had been shots he'd heard.

He was dizzy with pain and with the effort of concentrating. Yet suddenly he saw the whole thing, clear as spring water. Stryker had wanted him out of the way so he could betray the Occaneechi. Stryker, who had been friendly with the Senecas and in the woods had promised them some kind of reward—Stryker, whom he'd

never trusted. Stryker had lead the Senecas through Delk's un-
guarded part of the camp against the unarmed and helpless Occaneechi.

That was what all the yelling and firing was about. A battle was
underway, a battle in which the visiting Indians didn't stand a
chance because Ranger Delk Rogers had fallen for Stryker's trick.
Once again he had failed.

Delk managed at last to stagger to his feet though his head felt as
though it would fall from his shoulders. He drew a deep breath of the
cool air and closed his eyes. That seemed to steady him. Grip-
ping his carbine he started slowly across the savannah toward the
Occaneechi camp. He saw that one of the marquees was ripped to
ribbons, the other in flames. He passed two Indians still and crum-
pled on the ground.

A ranger shot by, only partly dressed, but fully armed. The fort
was awake now, as was Saponi Town. But they'd all be too late to
help. Stryker and his Indians had done their damage and gone.

Hanging White Man stood in the middle of the camp doing what
looked like a slow dance of rage, stamping and hopping about the
fire and shaking his fists in the direction of Christanna. A little way
beyond him the rest of the Occaneechi huddled together. Now
they were joined by the Saponi, running up from their village to
stand sleepily around the edge of the light.

Where was Jamie? Delk wondered. Had Stryker treated Pigg to
a hard wallop over the head too? He circled the camp to the spot
where Jamie had been guarding and looked around. There was no
sign of the jockey. Maybe he had been scared by the noise and shots
and had run into the woods. He might even have gone after the attacking Indians and was now chasing them through the woods
bravely. Delk's foot struck something metal and he stooped to see.

It was Jamie's carbine with the stock shattered. He'd fought and
been captured then! The Indians had the little jockey, and he'd probably died a hundred times of fright by now. Holding onto the gun,
he ran back to the Occaneechi camp. Captain Flood was standing
there, waving his arms and issuing orders, but Hanging White Man
was outshouting him.

"No good white men!" he bellowed. "Take Injuns guns, take Injuns bullets. No can fight, no guns. Fool warriors come. Steal Hanging White Man's son. Kill my people. Wicked, wicked! You no go to heb'm. Trick Injun. Wicked white men."

"Where's Captain Captain?" yelled the commander.

"They took him," answered a ranger. "The Senecas got him first off. Leonard Peacepipe's here, though."

Leonard Peacepipe was Captain Captain's brother. He stepped forward now, gun in hand.

"Leonard, tell Hanging White Man this was not any of our doings," Flood pleaded. "Tell him we are his friends. Tell him the rangers would never go back on their word to be friends."

He turned, "Proctor, go get their guns out of my office."

Hanging White Man listened to Leonard translate. Then he resumed his ranting, "Snake tongue, no tell truth. Take warpath against you. Have many friends. Friends help."

"Tell him, Leonard, tell him we did not betray him," Flood begged. "We mean to bring his son back and avenge his warrior's deaths. Tell him he's welcome to come fight with us against these Senecas."

Proctor returned with the guns and the Occaneechi braves sullenly snatched them up. Leonard started to explain, but the chief cut him short. "Take warriors home," he snarled. "Go on warpath. Sneaky white men. Kill my son. I kill you. Wicked, wicked."

Captain Flood rushed forward and tried to get one of the braves to put down his musket. "Stop them, stop them!" he cried to Leonard Peacepipe. "Tell them it's not our fault. Tell them quick."

The Occaneechi paid no heed but gathered up their few belongings. At last Hanging White Man picked up his gun and led them off through the woods.

The commander looked despairing. "We'll have to find that chief's boy and bring him back," he said flatly. "Leonard, get your best scouts and fighters. We need you. The rangers ride in an hour."

The Saponi drifted away and still the commander stood there looking about him in a dazed fashion. "Stryker?" he called. "Where's Stryker?" No one knew. "Don't tell me he's been shot. Don't tell me he's been captured too?"

"No, he ain't been none of those things," Delk bawled out. "He's a traitor and started all this. He hit me on the head and led the Senecas into camp. And he and his Seneca friends took Jamie Pigg off." He branished the jockey's carbine, then threw it angrily from him.

Flood looked astonished. "This ain't no time to come bearing false witness," he said.

"It's the truth," cried Delk. "It's the Gospel truth. He knocked me over the head. See here," and he showed the lump.

"He's got a fierce knot on his head, for sure," Hurdly said. "And it's mighty strange how them Senecas knew just when to come to Christanna for scalps and just where to attack the camp."

The commander shook his head. "We'll have to settle all that later," he spoke. "Not now. Hurdly, I'll need your help, Stryker's gone. Get 'em ready to ride in an hour." And he turned and stumbled blindly toward the fort.

It took however more than an hour to get the rangers ready. The men were armed, saddled and ready to mount in jig time. But one of the horses broke loose and went galloping out of the fort and had to be chased through the woods. When he was finally caught, he had lost a shoe. Some of the Saponi scouts were out fishing and had to be located. Captain Flood could not find the key to the powder room, and it was assumed that Stryker had taken it with him. Only after the door was forced did the commander recall that he had slid the key into his boot for safekeeping when he first heard the shots at the Indian camp.

Tupper poulticed Delk's head with warm wet bran and one of the Saponi cooks fixed him a noggin of something hot to drink. But by this time he was so worried about Jamie that he hardly noticed whether he was in pain or not. He couldn't stand to think about Jamie tortured by the fiendish Senecas, and he kept urging everyone to hurry, hurry, before it was too late.

At last they rode out, a grim group in the new cool light of a winter morning already slipping through the trees. They stopped to wait for the Saponi scouts to collect at the gate of the town. Delk groaned at the delay.

"Don't worry so," advised Hurdly. "We'll bring the little fellow back. Ten braves are already ahead, tracking the war party. We'll waste no time once we're under way."

"It was all my fault," said Delk. "I knew Stryker was up to something. I should have been more alert. I fell for his silly trick like some new-hatched gosling. I reckon he knew me well enough. Or his friends did."

He cut his eye around at Hurdly and suddenly shut up, setting his mouth in a stern line. Hurdly saw the look.

"Now wait a minute," the ranger exclaimed. "I wasn't in on Stryker's scheme. Not that maybe I wouldn't have gone along if he'd asked me," he added thoughtfully and then grinned. "But he never asked me. 'Struth. I figured he's found a lead mine, from hints he let drop and the surveying he was always doing here and there. I was hoping to be part of it. But not this other you tell about. I don't hold with setting Injuns against Injuns and getting a lot of white men scalped and killed. Especially not friends of mine, like Pigg."

Delk's heart warmed. Oh, Jamie would be pleased to know Hurdly counted him as a friend. Delk was glad enough to believe that Hurdly wasn't in on Stryker's plot. He liked Hurdly, in a way, and wouldn't relish thinking of him as a traitor.

Because Stryker was a traitor. Delk realized now that Stryker had had it in mind to use the Seneca to harry the peaceful Saponi till they deserted their reservation and fled elsewhere to safety. Then he and his important friend could file patents for it, but how they'd get the Council to approve such a huge grant of land, Delk didn't know. The scheme was bound to involve trickery for if there was a way to cheat folks Stryker would find it.

Nuck stumbled as they started off and the jolt sent a stab of pain through Delk's head. He'd dearly love to catch up with Stryker before this day was done. He'd fix him, not only for this knot, but for taking Pigg. Poor Jamie, Delk prayed that he wasn't suffering too much.

For a while they went at a fast pace, but then they slowed to allow the scouts time to make sure the war party hadn't left the well-worn path they were following. "It'll never do for us to lose them Senecas," Flood said as the rangers sat their horses waiting for the Saponi to conclude their search. "Somewhere they'll try to trick us. We must be on the watch."

Delk wished that they would hurry. He couldn't sit still thinking about Jamie being burned and cut by the Senecas and his skin peeled away in strips. He glanced around at the seven rangers and the little group of Saponi braves guarding the rear. Were there enough to fight the war party? Nobody knew how many Senecas had attacked. Even with the advanced scouts they didn't have more than twenty-five fighters all together. He shook his head, they'd never rescue Jamie, he knew.

Now they pushed on. Delk wondered if Stryker was really fleeing with the war party. He wouldn't mind having the chance to skewer Stryker's gizzard on his sword. He touched his waist to make sure he had his sword, and he checked to make sure he had all his other weapons too. It was certainly a lot, much too much for him to handle with ease. Hurdly had even made him fetch along extra cartridges. In his heart of hearts he was a little frightened. This would be his first battle, and he couldn't help speculating on whether he could use all that gear in proper fashion, at least expertly enough to come out alive.

As the morning passed and they still pressed on, Delk relaxed somewhat. He fastened his sword to the pommel and holding his carbine across his lap, he slumped in the saddle, trying to be patient and not fret at every stop the commander ordered, or every time they waited for the Indians. By midafternoon he was getting stiff and sore and he was sure they were on a fool's errand. Likely the Saponi had missed the point where the war party had left the path and now they'd go clip-clopping on and on, while Jamie was being hacked to ribbons, he told himself hopelessly.

They rode through thickets and across Indian old fields, now grown up to grass and young scrub pines. The land was hilly and often the way wound between great rocks. It looked desolate in the gray afternoon light with the leaves gone from the trees. An occasional pine grove was almost like a burst of sunlight, the color was so bright.

Then they reached a clearing, ringed mostly by thick trees and undergrowth, but on one side a little stream flowed and beyond its mossy banks there was a slope, thick with gnarled sumac bushes, with a scattering of boulders. After quick glances at the ground the scouts passed across the clearing. The rangers clopped slowly along behind and were in the middle of the opening when the first shot was fired.

Delk stopped, surprised. For a moment all the rangers sat their horses as if they were frozen. The slope was suddenly filled with white puffs. Bullets whined past. From all sides guns cracked and war whoops sounded. Ambushed! They had been ambushed good and proper!

The commander's horse reared as Flood tried to unsheath his sword. Hurdly had already wheeled and was headed up the slope, when Flood raised himself in the stirrups and with sword held over his head, yelled, "Charge! No quarter!"

Delk slung the carbine strap around his shoulder, unfastened the pistol-holster flaps, and turned Nuck all at the same time, it seemed to him. He kicked the horse in the sides and galloped through the branch and up the rise. He slipped out his sword. It was heavy and leaden in his hand and though he held it pointed before him, he wasn't sure he'd be able to use it. But he couldn't put it back for the scabbard had bounced from the pommel.

An Indian rose up before him with a musket aimed straight at him. He crouched behind Nuck's head and rode right toward him. The Seneca fired and ducked as Delk swung the sword in a wide arc, missing the brave by inches. Delk snatched out a pistol and turning in the saddle shot. The Indian continued to reload his gun.

Delk grabbed the reins and guided Nuck around and charged back at the Seneca. He'd missed him twice and he didn't aim to do so again. The Indian looked around just as Delk reached him but was too late to ward off the jab of the long blade. It went into his chest and for a moment he ran alongside before Delk was able to free the sword.

An arrow plinked into the saddle by his leg. He looked around and saw Flood go down with an arrow in his side. Tupper rushed to help him. Hurdly was riding back and forth slashing and yelling. One of his sleeves was stained with blood.

Nearby Proctor's horse blowing red froth from its lips reared and pawed the air, wild with pain. The ranger fell as his mount bolted forward and he was unable to clear his foot from the stirrup. He went bouncing along through bushes and whacking against rocks.

Delk rushed forward and with a slash of the sword cut the stirrup strap. Proctor jumped up and unslung his carbine and with a "Thanks, youngster!" sprinted toward some rocks, where Captain Flood was propped up, shooting and calmly reloading and shooting again.

Delk wasn't sure they weren't taking a licking. Only five rangers still mounted, and where were the Saponi? Had they fled at the first sound of firing? Most of the Indians he saw were stripped and circled with paint, and the hillside seemed alive with them.

He sent Nuck galloping, headed for a kneeling gunman. He got ready to lean out and swing his sword, but Nuck didn't swerve. His hoofs sent the Indian sprawling. Looking back, Delk didn't see the brave rise, and he rode on. An arrow grazed the top of his leg, tearing his pants and embedding itself in the saddle. He pulled it loose and raced on.

Suddenly a huge painted warrior leaped from behind a rock with a broad-bladed spear. Before Delk could rein Nuck away, the Indian had rushed in close and ripped open the horse's belly and slashed across the thigh. Nuck screamed and went rolling over. Delk tried to kick his feet free of the stirrup and leap away, but one leg was caught under the dying animal and he hit the ground with a tremendous thump.

The warrior bounded onto Nuck's side and with both hands raised his spear high overhead.

## Chapter 14

# Scalps

The Seneca's foot slipped on Nuck's bloody side and he tee-
tered backward, struggling to regain his balance. In that moment Delk sat up and stabbed with the sword, feeling it slice
into the Indian's thigh. Nuck whinnied piteously and struggled to
rise, and Delk jerked his leg free as the warrior lunged down with
the great-bladed dart.

The spear plunged into the earth as Delk rolled to one side.
Snatching at the wooden shaft, the Seneca still kept his eyes on the
boy. Delk leaped to his feet and at the same time slashed out with
his sword. The blade missed the savage's arm but whacked through
the wooden shaft. Delk's feet had gotten mixed up he had swung so
quickly and he tottered, off balance.

As he struggled to straighten up and strike again, the Seneca
knocked the sword from his hand. With a triumphant cry the brave
grabbed it by the hilt and stood. He faced the boy and a look of evil
joy slid across his face as he hefted the sword and tensed to spring.

Delk had no intention of falling under his very own weapon. He
backed off, wondering frantically where his carbine had fallen.
There was no time to look for it. He'd have to try for the pistol in
his saddle holster.

Whirling, he vaulted over Nuck and fumbled at the flap. For a
moment he thought the pistol had jogged from the holster when
Nuck fell, but then his fingers closed over the butt and panic left

him. He dropped to one knee, rested his arm along the horse's side and aimed carefully at the charging Seneca. He fired and the warrior jerked up short, half turned and fell in a heap. The sword dropped with a metallic sound.

Delk flung the pistol from him. He'd never liked shooting it and with more fighting to do, he wanted his carbine. He found the gun in the bushes and with it before him he circled the Indian cautiously. The Seneca lay still, his body twisted and bloody. The boy moved over to his horse and gave it a sad pat.

"Good old Nuck," he said. "You done fine for just a harrow horse. Just fine."

Now Delk made his way to where Tupper sat on the ground trying to pull an arrow from his shoulder. "Dern fool Injuns," he snarled. "Why can't they shoot a man with a decent lead ball. I can't fight with this thing sticking out of me."

Delk tried to pull it out but couldn't. "Here," Tupper said, handing him a knife, "cut the shaft off close as you can. Somebody can dig the flint head out later. There's more fighting to do." He looked around and added, "I do believe we'll rout the varmints."

Delk did as he was told and handed back the knife. "Do you want me to bandage it?"

"No time for that," Tupper said, getting to his feet. "Proctor needs help. Come on."

Delk ran after him. Ahead of them with his back to a boulder Proctor held two braves at bay by swinging his carbine back and forth. The Indians were armed with slender scalping knives, and they edged in closer and then pulled back as the gunstock came toward them.

Tupper gave a yell. "Hang on, Proctor!"

One of the Indians feinted and Proctor swung and the other brave leaned forward and sank his knife into the ranger's stomach. Proctor fell back against the rock, beating at the Seneca weakly, and the other Indian knocked the gun from his grasp. The ranger put his hands to his wound and blood gushed in great torrents between his fingers. He slumped to the ground.

The brave gave a wild flourish of his bloody knife and, crouching, skulked away among the bushes. Tupper stopped and aimed his carbine at the departing warrior. He fired and the Seneca stumbled. "I'll finish him off," he yelled to Delk, bounding down the slope. "Don't let that other 'un take Proctor's scalp. Whatever you do, don't let him have it."

The Seneca dropped astride Proctor and began to circle the crown of the ranger's head with his knife. Delk aimed his gun and fired but the flint snapped on an empty pan. He flung the carbine at the Indian in disgust and, shouting, began to run forward again.

The warrior looked around contemptuously and then with deliberate calm put his foot on Proctor's head, gave a hard pull, and scalped him. He held up his trophy and screamed, a long triumphant shriek. Shaking it at Delk, he sped around the rock and up the hill.

Delk followed up the slope. He didn't aim to let the Seneca get away. No ranger had ever lost his scalp to the red man. It was a matter of honor. Especially for poor Proctor who had always worried that he would wake up on Judgment Day minus an arm or some other part of his body and have to do without it forever. Now Delk meant to see that his hair was buried with him.

He hadn't known how tired he was till he tried to speed up that rise. He could hardly keep his legs pumping. He stripped off his empty cartouche box as he ran and it helped some not to have it flapping against his side.

The warrior had disappeared over the top of the hill. When Delk reached the brow he couldn't see the fleeing Indian anywhere. There was a little grove of pines ahead of him growing above a narrow ravine, filled with dry brush and leaves, almost as if someone had deliberately dumped it there. Suddenly an Indian stepped from among the pines with wads of burning grass in his hand. He paused a moment to glance over his shoulder at Delk and then he threw these torches into the ravine. He went up and down the little wash, throwing in the brands. The man was mad. Why stop to burn brush here and now?

Then Delk heard clearly a familiar voice. "Oh, 'elp! 'elp!" It was Jamie. "Don't let me burn. Somebody 'elp!"

Jamie! He must be under the burning leaves and grass. He'd be roasted. With a yell Delk sprinted forward right into the fire. The Seneca stared at him in astonishment and turning fled back among the trees.

The grass and leaves caught immediately and the flames were

waist high. Delk gasped as he waded into the blaze, not able to see or hear and surrounded by the terrifying, licking, leaping tongues of fire. In a second or two the driest stuff had burned off, and the brush underneath had caught and was crackling fiercely in several places. Panic-stricken, Delk kicked and knocked the burning sticks aside. The smoke was sharp and scalding, his eyes ran with tears, his hands were already blistered.

"Jamie, Jamie!" he bawled. "Where are you?"

His hand struck something, a moccasined foot and he hauled the man out by his legs. It was Captain Captain bound hand and foot and the thong looped so tight around his neck he couldn't move. He looked half dead. Delk snatched out his knife and cut the bindings. Captain Captain staggered to his feet and began to beat at the flames with a pine branch.

Under a layer of burning cane they came on Hanging White Man's son, half suffocated. Jamie yelled again and Delk answered. The fire was mounting and roaring and the heat almost too great to bear. Where was Jamie, where was Jamie?

"Help, help," Delk screamed, not knowing what he was saying, and Jamie answered right under his feet. " 'Elp! 'Elp! I'm on fire, I'm on fire."

Delk reached down into the blaze and grabbed an arm and hauled the little man out. His shirt was on fire and Captain Captain and Delk beat it out and pulled him up the side of the ravine before they cut his bonds. Delk was breathing in great gasps and the other three seemed too frightened and dazed and horror stricken to speak.

The fire in the ravine spent itself at last and now was only blue smoke and an occasional crackle and sputter. The battle must be over; there were no shots or yells that Delk could hear. He lay back on the bed of fallen pine needles and struggled to fill his lungs with air.

Captain Captain touched him on the shoulder. Instead of being a fine bronzy brown the way it usually was, his skin was sort of gray. "Hands much burned," spoke the Saponi. "Alive, alive. Amen, amen."

The young Occaneechi sat up and inspected a large blister on his shoulder and some cuts on his legs. He looked up at Delk and his eyes were somber and brooding. All at once he smiled. "You much good. Good for white man. You friend." He nodded twice firmly and then went back to his thoughts.

Delk turned his head to look at Pigg. With a startled cry he sprang up. He'd been too late, they'd already scalped the poor little man. Captain Captain sprang up too as Delk knelt beside Jamie. "What've they done to you?" he cried. "What's the matter with your head?"

Jamie grinned and touched the big dirty mass of his head. "It's only mud," he replied wryly. "They plastered me 'ead with mud afore they put us in the brush."

"Save scalp," explained Captain Captain. "Hid us there." He pointed to the ravine. "Come get after battle. Take us away to Seneca town, cut up in little pieces."

He laughed as though he thought this was a fine notion. "But rangers come," he went on. "Whip Senecas, whip Senecas good. So burn us there. Only hope for red hair scalp. Put on mud, scalp not burn. Senecas come back after and find it."

Delk took a minute to figure this out. It had been clever of the Senecas to secrete their prisoners in the ravine during the ambush and battle. That way they had counted on claiming their victims if the battle had gone in their favor. If the whites won, still the three prisoners would die a ghastly death before the remnant of Senecas fled. And who but a Seneca would think of plastering Jamie's hair with clay so that even after he was dead of burning they could find his shining hair and carry it back to the village in triumph. A scalp like that was rare indeed.

Once again Delk wondered if Stryker had been with the Senecas and had helped to plan this bit of meanness. Surely even Stryker couldn't take part in such cruelty to another white man. Still there was a deal of money involved, and Delk knew that better men than Stryker had forgotten their humanity for that much money.

It had been a bad day all around. It was almost dark, and the shadows seemed to Delk evil and threatening. Suddenly he wanted light and company and protection, for none of them had a weapon.

He started off and Jamie got to his feet. "Come along," Delk said. "Let's go find a ranger or two, if they're still alive. And something to eat."

# Chapter 15

# Farewell to Fort Christanna

elk stood outside his barracks filling his lungs with the sharp, sweet December air. It was a clear night with no smell of snow for tomorrow. The stars overhead were cold, brittle points of light, but the evening star shone calm and warm and bright. Tomorrow he would be heading in that direction and who knew how far west that beckoning star might lead him? An owl called softly and he hoped it was a good luck sign.

Christanna was quiet. A light came from the cracks around the Indian company's headquarters door. Captain Hix had been instructed to hang on, though the company seemed doomed to cease operations. It was the center of much squabbling between the House of Burgesses and Governor Spotswood, but no one expected the Governor to win out and keep the company in operation.

But the light that shone from the Reverend Griffin's door was more hopeful. His salary was paid by Spotswood from the Governor's own purse, and he'd be here to see to the Indian children's education no matter what happened. Hanging White Man's son, Occaneechi Boy, was staying in the building, and the teacher was even now this night still instructing him in the Christian religion.

Delk flexed his hands and then scraped at a little dried skin on his palm. Whatever Occaneechi Boy had used for medicine, it had proved most effective. All of Delk's burns had healed quickly and well. Jamie had had a mite more trouble, for his back had been more severely scorched, but even he, before he rode off to Williamsburg, had seemed recovered and unbothered.

Delk shook his head sadly. It depressed him to think he'd never see his copper-haired friend again. He had begged Jamie over and over to stay in the colonies and go trading or just stay and try some work or other. Pigg had stubbornly declined. He had left with Captain Flood and some of the others when the rangers were dissolved. Now all were gone.

Captain Flood had gone to Williamsburg, no doubt to revel in balls and parties and tell of great ranger skirmishes and stirring patrols. Tupper had gone to his home and Hurdly to his. Hurdly had promised to stop off on way to calm Delk's four sisters and tell them their brother would visit them next spring. Jamie had left for his ship. Proctor had gone to his grave without his scalp. Stryker had not been seen or heard of since the attack on the Occaneechi camp, but word had been spread to beware of this man as a traitor. The other rangers had scattered to the winds.

"I wonder if I'll ever see any of them again?" Delk mused. Surely he would, sometime, somewhere.

Well, no matter. Tomorrow he'd leave Fort Christanna as a trader, a thing he'd never thought of last summer before he became a ranger. All his fortune had taken a strange and wonderful turn since then.

He stepped back inside the empty barracks. A fire burned on the hearth and a single candle on the table lit up the assortment of trade goods spread about the room. The wavering light glinted on the knife blades and the hoe blades, the satiny surface of the bright ribbons, and the gold thread running through the lace on one of the coats. Delk picked it up, a double-striped cloth coat laced with tinsel. It was very fine, and he slipped it on and admired himself. He strode around the room and then bowed gravely to a bench, remembering how his sisters had taught him to sweep off his hat and make obeisance to a lady.

"At your service," he said aloud and then straightened up with a grin.

The coat was not really his, it was a gift from Captain Hix to Hanging White Man, just as a good many of the fine things spread out here were gifts to the Occaneechi. Captain Hix was doing all he knew how to keep the uncertain peace on this frontier. Already Captain Captain had sent two runners to assure Hanging White Man that his son was safe, that the white rangers had done all they could to avenge the sneak attack, and that Occaneechi Boy would soon be returned to them along with many gifts.

It was Captain Hix who had wanted some ranger to accompany Occaneechi Boy back to his village. Even before they'd all left he had come straight to Delk and said, "Rogers, you was the one who saved this lad, you're bound to be the one to honor him home." He cleared his throat. "I had my doubts about you, at times, Rogers, but you've made a good ranger, I wager, and no doubt to my mind about that. You've quitted yourself like a man these perilous months and I know I can trust you with this mission."

Delk couldn't help but be pleased. He knew the Captain was flattering him, but at the same time he knew there was considerable truth in what he said. The careless boy who had reported here, not even able to keep up with his own cap, had disappeared in these months. He could be trusted! He knew it and he was glad Captain Hix knew it. But what a responsibility rested on his shoulders.

Traders fleeing back here from the Carolina wilderness told of towns preparing to go on the warpath to help their Occaneechi friends and kinsmen, of day and night dances to arouse war fervor, and of Indians sullen and mean, demanding that all white men be killed and burned. No longer did traders leave Christanna for far-off towns, no longer did friendly Indians come here to trade, lest they too be attacked by their enemies while unarmed.

Some white man had to go to the Occaneechi chief with gifts and the scalps of the Seneca taken in that battle, and with his son. Someone had to placate him and try to keep him from stirring up the other tribes and other towns into following him on the warpath against Virginia. With the rangers no longer around for frontier protection and with the trading facilities of Christanna doomed any day, something had to be attempted to protect the settlers and the friendly Indians along the southern border of Virginia. And that something had to be quick, for there was no time to wait for burgesses and other governing officials to bicker among themselves long enough to come to a decision.

Tomorrow Delk would set out. Captain Captain would act as an intermediary, making speeches and presenting the scalps and the gifts, and Occaneechi Boy had promised to help placate his father and keep him from going on the warpath. Delk had hoped Jamie Pigg would be with him to help with the horses, and he had begged and begged him. The jockey had said no and ridden off to Williamsburg with Captain Flood.

He shrugged now. Even without Jamie he had a lot to look forward to. Occaneechi Boy had promised if the meeting with his father went well, that then he would lead Delk into the high mountains to see what was to be seen, and would go with him on westward to the other side where the buffalo spotted the meadows "as many as leaves on a tree." Delk's heart gave a great leap at these words, and he knew he'd take almost any risk to have such a dream come true.

Now he stared down at the goods on the barracks table and grabbed up a sash. "A red girdle, two skins," he said aloud. "A brass kettle, that's three skins."

How strange it sounded to be Delk Rogers, Indian trader. But that was what he was. He'd taken his ranger pay and bought vermilion paint, strouds, knives, caddis lace, and all kinds of other truck. These items he would barter beyond the mountains when he and Occaneechi Boy explored there.

It was wonderful and exciting to be going into those far rich, wild lands beyond the mountains. Captain Hix had given him a strong, short-legged, ugly creature named Poppy for no reason that Delk could figure. She would make a fine pack horse and with the others he was borrowing, a fine string of loaded animals would leave tomorrow morning.

"But I'll miss poor old Nuck," he thought. "Nuck wasn't just a horse—he was a friend."

He walked over and poked the fire. It was lonely in the barracks. He added another log. The fire sputtered as it sprang up. A spider ran out from among the kindling at the side of the hearth and slid between the cracks in the floor.

There was a sudden sound outside, a distant clop of horse's hoofs. Delk raised his head and listened. Who could be riding in after dark this way? Had someone come to warn the fort that after all the Indians were taking the warpath? Had someone come from the Occaneechi towns to snatch Occaneechi Boy away? Was it the Senecas attacking again?

At this moment he sprang up and ran to the door, but even before he got there, it swung open and a voice cried, "Oh, blimy, I'm froze. Stir up the fire, Delk, me lad, and let's 'ave something to eat."

"Jamie!" bawled Delk, "Jamie Pigg! Whatever are you doing here?"

The tiny man grinned, almost wide enough to stretch from wall to wall. "I come back," he said simply. "I come back to tell you I changed me mind. I'll go with ye among the blasted 'eathen savages."

Delk could hardly believe his ears. He seized the jockey by the shoulders and danced across the floor with him. "You're a liar," he cried. "You don't really mean it?"

"Solemn truth," replied Jamie gravely. "I done paid out my money for a pretty good 'orse, and I come back to go journeying with you."

"Well, how come?" Delk asked grinning and dancing about the Englishman. "Oh, I'm proud to have you, Jamie. But how come you waited till now?"

Jamie sat down on a bench and scratched his red head. "Well, I don't rightly know," he admitted at last. "I just kept thinking about that ship and 'ow I 'ated to cross the water. And about London and 'ow maybe it'd be pretty dull there. And 'ow I was 'eaded for being too old to ride in them races. They jog a body up terribly, they do.

"And I thought about you, Delk, and 'ow you was good to me, ever, and 'ow it wouldn't be right to let you go alone into the wilderness, for I knew you'd need somebody along to remind you to fetch your 'ead along, in case it should come unfastened from your shoulders!"

Delk gave him a friendly shove, and cried, "That ain't so any longer and, you know, I've learned to watch my ways and do what I'm supposed to do." Then in case Jamie should think he didn't want him, he added hastily, "Most of the time anyhow."

Jamie grinned in his turn. "And I thought about all the things that had 'appened to me," he went on. "And it come to me that I was over the worst. I been 'alf-et by a bear and I been well nigh roasted alive and still 'ere I be, alive and jumping. I figured the Lord saved me to go and tend to your pack animals—what do you know about 'andling 'orses?"

He was right, Delk thought. Just as he had learned not to be so thoughtless, so Jamie had learned not to be fearful. Here he had ridden alone and in the dark woods back to the fort this very night. That must have taken courage for Jamie Pigg.

"Ah, that's so," Delk said aloud. "The bad things have happened and now there's nothing ahead of us but good things, Jamie, a whole wide world of good things, and we'll start for them tomorrow!"

"Now ain't that grand?" Jamie spoke dreamily. "A 'ole wide world!" And he and Delk stared together into the fire. Tomorrow— a whole wide world!